WICKED PURSUITS

Dear CC, we aren't there doesn't mean we never will be. Let's keep walking.

WICKED PURSUITS

ADITYA SHAKALYA

PARTRIDGE
A Penguin Random House Company

To order additional copies of this book, contact
Partridge India
000 800 10062 62
orders.india@partridgepublishing.com

www.partridgepublishing.com/india

CONTENTS

ACKNOWLEDGEMENT

A finished book is the culmination of efforts put in by various people playing different roles in the life of an author; if one of these misfires the story can be stalled for years to come. This story wouldn't have been possible without the critical inputs of Harshita, my wife, who gave me time and peace when I needed it the most to pamper my creative juices. It was her trust in my writing and constant interrogation about how much of the book is remaining that helped me cross the finish line without slacking (too much).

I was lucky to have two sets of parents, Sadhna & Vijay (mine) and Namita & Vasu (Harshita's) who (irrationally) have always treated me like a star and this book is a small homage to their unquestioned love and trust.

I'll be forever indebted to Ta for the support and for enabling the release of this book in time.

A shout out to all the friends Sha, Ju, Lata, Husain and Purva (my lovely niece) for sportingly being the target of my jokes and remarks, you have unknowingly been the catalyst in moving the story forward.

A special mention of the entire Kakwani clan (Kalanis and Motawanis included) for taking my mind off the burner every now and then; your company always leaves me invigorated (and with a slight headache).

Thanks Shweta and Ginni for diligently going through the manuscript and spotting errors; now you are stuck with doing this before every release.

Finally, no acknowledgement list of mine can be complete without Carlos-my elder son, who will never read my book (being an English bulldog) but who can teach many a men about friendship, love and loyalty. He has prevented me from exploding on various occasions and is my silent (and perpetually hungry) support.

Kaizen (my two month old son, a human), I hope this book is worth showing off to your friends once you grow up.

TALE OF THE TALE

I ndia, the 'popular third world' country is changing faster every day than it did in all these years since independence. Various developments around the world have opened doors for those who want to go up in life, the means are many.

The lopsided distribution of authority and the consequential surge in incidents of brazen corruption have bestowed so much power in the hands of the few that the traditional gang lords have been replaced by such poster children for growth (albeit for few) and their ambitious, subservient thugs who have no qualms about putting the country up for ransom if it serves their purpose.

The story is of some such men and their desires.

CHAPTER 1

FUCK IT!

He just lay there on the couch, slouching, a quarter sitting and three quarters prostrate with the remote on his stomach. The television was on but accidently muted when he shifted his butt to look for the remote to change the channel. But he forgot why had he needed the remote in the first place, which show had he planned to watch? Should have set a reminder, he pondered; although the silence was not all that bad; he could hear himself munching on *sev parmal*, chomp chomp chomp, he enjoyed the sound for a while and then got irritated with it so he turned the volume back up. According to the countdown timer on the screen, 1.30 minutes were left before the movie resumed; just about enough to surf through few channels but what if he found something else to watch on the other channel and forgot that he was watching a movie and then by the time he would realize it would be too late and he will miss that sequence where those reinvigorated hockey playing girls beat up the teasing guys at McDonalds, he found that sequence unbelievable but funny nonetheless. Anyway, like a neat trick by a street magician, the verdict had made itself evident now, no decision needed to be taken; it was only 5 seconds before the movie would begin. What a waste of time, he halfheartedly reprimanded himself wiping the *Chaat masala* off his hands on his vest. It was only 2:00 PM, dad was at work, and mother had gone to her room to take an afternoon nap after feeding him the mundane lunch about which he didn't complain anymore. Still four hours before dad got back home and he'll have to look busy doing things that busy people do, what would those be today? He will try and figure out around 5:30.

Mom got up at 3:30, it was time to start preparations for evening snacks once the sole earner of the family gets back and then dinner almost soon after. *Nashta* they call it in Hindi, a common word for breakfast, mid-day snacks and everything in between, unlike English speaking folk there is no distinction between meals based on the time of day it is eaten, perhaps that's why the older generation, that could only speak functional English to barely get by in an increasingly Anglicized India and to not be considered a fool by its own kids who spoke English 'just like an American' (they thought), frequently talked about dinner at noon and lunch after the 8:00 PM sitcom and had breakfast multiple times a day. His derailed train of thought was broken by mom's call for tea and her almost supernatural confiscation of the remote. It was the sleight of hand only his mom could execute and before he realized, he was watching a show full of women with flaring *Sarees* only matched by their nostrils that flared while they planned the downfall of some man for something he or his family shouldn't have done. Ah! *Chai*, good old Indian tea, much better than the milk-less tea the *firangs* drank with all the pomp and show, was the only high point of the day so far, after hot *Samosa* that he had for breakfast of course. "*Beta*, we are almost out of salt, get some from the store nearby." she calmly passed the order. Might as well do what mom says, he thought, who knows there may be some looker at the store also obeying her mother's orders. The store was not too far away and he decided to take a walk; funny, this thing, salt, too little or too much and food becomes inedible, too little or too much in the body and there are medical complications. How the hell are you supposed to eat that grainy powder in a way that it is just right. Fuck it! All of us are going to die anyway. 'Fuck it', the term much loathed by those who could only understand it in one way, was the protection mechanism that his brain had adapted over time, almost like a survival strategy; if things became too profound to think through or too complicated to hinder an instant judgment, they were dismissed with the use of this phrase. Buying salt was pretty uneventful, no woman, let alone pretty, could be seen anywhere in the store or outside. Doesn't matter, he was anyway not dressed for such a chanced occasion, better to have no impression than a bad one, he mulled. With the remaining money, he bought a can of Coke, just to pass time. Coca Cola! What a company, selling just brown, sugared water for so many years, making millions, and here I stand contributing my thirty rupees to their growing balances. What if we stop drinking this ….Fuck it!

———◆•◆•◆———

Eye of the tiger! His cell phone played a shrill rendition of the soundtrack from the immensely popular (among boys) movie. It was 6 AM, time to hit the gym and get ripped. What better way to start a day being inspired by a fictional boxer! He got up, had a glass of water and went to the washroom. Damn, my left knee is hurting, he acknowledged, must be because of the heavy leg workout I did last week, this could aggravate if I don't give it a chance to heal; "Maa I am going back to sleep, don't make the banana shake." he yelled and got back in bed falling asleep instantly only to wake up at 10. He could have woken up earlier, but it is better to make sure that dad is not around before or after doing something unproductive, anyway he didn't want to argue with him in the morning, it only spoiled the rest of his day.

———◆•◆•◆———

Hearing some commotion in the room and a definite sound of the flush, mom yelled from the kitchen, "Are you up? Breakfast is on the table". He blithely had the *Aaloo Paratha* while checking text messages, making sure that his expressions do not give him away. It was 11 already, time to meet up a couple of friends, one who had come down from Delhi for a few days and the other who had begun working in the town itself but had taken a leave on account of a broken toe. He picked up his (dad's old) bike and left for the tea stall that was far enough from the house for anybody to come and check on them, soon the other two also reached, Ravi rode the gearless scooter while Praveen sat at the back with his broken toe highlighted by a plaster that pretty much covered the entire foot for better grip. *Kaalu*, buy us tea and Gold Flake, you are the only earning member here, he insisted after all of them settled on a narrow stone bench right next to a cemented water tank. Ravi, a name for the Sun in *Sanskrit*, was ironically dark skinned and had been baptized as *Kaalu* and other similar sounding variants since in school; he used to get offended earlier, resorting to fist fights and complains to the class teacher but as it happens in every healthy child's life, he had made peace with it and felt odd when his friends called him by his real name. "Why should it be me every time?" Ravi retorted, "Even *Takla* has a job now and he didn't even spend any money in traveling all the way from Delhi". Praveen had taken up after his father and was already balding, even before hitting twenty five; he getting a job had less to do with his desire to work and more to do with settling and finding a beautiful housewife for him before girls start rejecting him for having a receding hairline. The search was on full throttle but with him still single; his parents appeared to be fighting a losing battle. "Dude, I would have surely paid but right now all my money is being used up in going to the Hospital, next time the treat would be mine". "Of course it would be," interjected Karan, "but we need a full bottle of *Simran Oaf* every day from once the girl for you is finalized till you lock your room to make the poor girl a victim of your lust", they laughed. The time flew by, sitting, bantering, talking nothing about everything and still the sound never ceased. The topic of the day, however, was Karan's job. When asked by dad's friends or neighborhood aunties buying vegetables from the cart, he would give a vague response about not being interested or being selected already and just waiting for the offer letter, whatever he fancied at the moment, he made light of it with the friends as well but now that both of them were working, it was time to give one hard look at his resume and make it good enough to get accepted.

———◆•◆•◆———

CHAPTER 2

THE RELUCTANT SOLDIER

Karan was one of those who preferred sitting on the fence and not taking sides if he could help it. He was one of those who would always give a 'Can't Say' response to questions that required binary answers as either yes or no. He liked to think that he was an observer but if somebody would ask him to reflect upon his observation, he wouldn't really recall what the act was in the first place. He didn't like anything, he didn't dislike anything, neither did he love anything, nor did he hate anything. A science student, he decided to get into BBA because that was the in thing in those days. He didn't try for any entrance exams; not that he didn't appear in any, in India every kid worth his mother's milk appears in at least few of the examinations to secure one seat in a college his dad could be proud of. But he just appeared because everybody else was attempting and again, being found strolling on the roads when others were busy building their careers would be tough to defend.

When the results were out, Karan wasn't very optimistic, he couldn't decide if he had done well in the tests or not, his opinion about his own performance fluctuated with the mood of people around him; but there was no miracle, his roll number did not appear in any of those lists, a result that would have made the buttons pop out off the shirt of his father calmly eluded him. He could tell that his parents also did not have any high hopes from him, they never asked if he got through, knowing well that in the unlikely case of him clearing and beating thousands of other much more serious students, he would come himself and let them know about his act of valor, but that never happened.

A new trend had emerged in the days of aimless actions and self doubt; education had become a business worth pursuing and various colleges offering degrees from BA to MBBS had mushroomed across the country; for many like Karan who were neither talented nor outright dumb to get into an Arts College and neither exceptionally brilliant nor filthy rich to get into a Medical College, BBA was the degree to opt for. Bachelors in Business Administration, what an impressive sounding qualification, it was sure to make him and million others top class managers with packages that were sure to get them brides that were beauty pageant level pretty, 'Masterchef' level cooks, and daily soap level family *bahus.*

As an act of desperation, after predictably not getting through any of the prestigious exams while many others did and to avoid swipes by his father of ending up as a meager 'Twelfth Pass', Karan programmed himself to believe that BBA was the degree that would change his life, add to that, the lure of the promised land where movies made gullible youth believe that college life is where you find pretty girls and indifferent faculties who really would let you get away with murder as long as you could help the alma mater win some inter-institute competitions with your talent and charm, gave him a good enough reason to set his heart to the cause. Karan's father, a hard working man who never really achieved much in his own life, other than a stable job, didn't want much from his son. The initial euphoria of having a son who would be the next conquistador subsided pretty rapidly once he started attending school and turning up with strictly average results. So much for conquering the world; Mr. Surana sighed at some point in his early life as a father and dropped his arms acquiescing Karan to whatever his destiny had decided for him.

The girl sat across the counseling table with a black blazer and a very officious looking face, her makeup and demeanor made her look older than she was but added certain authority to her countenance. Politely yet firmly she talked to Karan and his father, mostly to his father, parroting stats that could have been just made up numbers to fool young, clueless kids and nervous parents into paying up the admission fee even before she concluded her spiel. But these numbers were real! They were written in a well designed and well printed brochure that had a picture of two girls attentively discussing something academic, standing in the lobby of a building that could have been this college. Behind them were the lush green lawns accommodating other students who were sitting in the grass so fresh that one could almost smell it off the paper! Those other students, though a little blurred, also looked busy and neat. Back at the desk, the girl was talking about the courses, the extracurricular activities and the world class faculty along with the fee structure, but in his head, Karan had already taken his admission there, he was walking through classrooms, sharing his desk with pretty girls and sitting in the lawn preparing for the exams with his friends, mostly girls, while munching on a value pack of *Kurkure*. "Any questions?" the girl counselor's gentle but business like voice disrupted his dream. Ummm, he tried to look as if he was in deep thought and about to come up with the smartest question ever asked on that table, fully aware that his dad looked at him with half boredom and half pessimism, already trying to calculate the dent his son's degree will make in his middle class bank account.

———◆•◆•◆———

The college was in the city, two hours from the suburban settlement where he lived. They took a bus back home, carrying a free bag gifted by the college with a proud logo screen printed on it. The bag contained the brochure, admission form and a water bottle they had carried from home. Why pay for ten rupees *ka* Bisleri when you can carry clean, cold water from home, the fact that the water becomes lukewarm within next half an hour of non-consumption and eventually undrinkable in such a long journey was a different matter. Dad sat in the aisle seat and dozed, perhaps thinking about a successful trip, the father in him rekindling dreams of a bright future for his son, Karan sitting next to him had already logged in to facebook through his phone that looked exactly like one of those expensive ones that cost more than his dad's monthly salary and liked the college's page. Various likes on random posts by female sounding names gave him new hope, may be this would be his time, his time to shine and be recognized for his talents that were not discovered yet, by others and by himself.

CHAPTER 3

MAMA I'M LEAVING HOME

The admission form had been filled and sent, a perfunctory acceptance letter was received, the first of its kind in the Surana house. Mom was happy, sure that things will be better now, relieved that the unsaid friction, the cold-war between the father and the son will be stalled for a while, if not permanently. Moreover, now she could answer to her friends and mothers of Karan's friends about her son's admission adding a little spice to the entire process. She can't be blamed, that is how mothers are, proud of their creation's smallest achievements and voluntarily ignorant of their shortcomings.

Finally the day arrived, to leave the comfortable confines of a small but warm house to the hostile walls of a smaller and unknown rented room that Karan was supposed to share with Yash Chaudhari. Yash belonged to the same town but had studied in a different school, Karan knew him from the playground days and from various stories that he had heard of him. Even his dad had heard about C.K. Chaudhari's son, mostly all bad things, the kind that made him worry for the gullible Karan even more. Both the father-son couple had crossed by each other at the bus depot, Karan's dad had seen Mr. Chaudhari walking ahead but he decided against calling him out, not that there was any enmity between the two, just that he did not want to waste time or miss the few remaining seats on the bus by indulging in some inconsequential small talk. The day after the counseling, it was Yash's mother, loud and rural even by the town's standards, who met Mrs. Surana near the dairy and told her about her son's admission. Simple women that they were, they both decided that their sons will stay in the same room and be brothers in arms in a fast paced city full of criminals and girls with lose character. Karan's dad did not take this new development well; when Lakshmi, his wife and Karan's mom, told him how Yash's mother had generously offered that their son could share the room with Yash, the room for which they had paid a six month's deposit already, he fumed and mumbled inaudible but understandable profanities, then turned to Karan who was pretending to watch TV with his ears firmly directed towards the other more important discussion and said, "Don't get influenced by your new friend, I know what kind of a guy he is". Karan just nodded, he knew dad was referring to Yash's smoking but knew his dad enough to not argue with him.

The day arrived and the Surana parents accompanied their son to the bus depot where Yash was already waiting for them, earphones in his ears, gum in his mouth, a bump in his chest pocket strongly indicative of a cigarette packet. Karan's dad instantly made a face depicting disgust but his mom, knowing her husband well, nudged him hard instinctively. "What kind of parents doesn't come to see their kids off?" he inaudibly mumbled. The farewell was quickly over, teary eyed mother hugged Karan and waved good bye, not planning to look weak while the dad patted both on the shoulders, "Don't do anything out of line, we would be visiting soon." They settled in their seats and it was time to leave.

Yash had been admitted in an institute that offered pharmacy related courses and was fifteen minutes away from Karan's college, but once the courses commenced both got busy with their lives and the only thing common between them was their home town and toilet in the apartment.

The first day of college was a bittersweet event for Karan and other gullible children like him; the college was not as big as they had thought it would be. What had appeared to be a sprawling lawn on the cover of the brochure was a small green patch near the canteen, or it could have been an image from the internet, maybe those girls also didn't belong to that college. All the classrooms were not as big as the one shown on the inside pages, some were small and stuffy with a window opening towards another wall of an adjoining construction. It was too early to find out if the number of placements were really as many as the institute claimed but fuck it, who had time to worry about such things, there were still few years to face the facts, this first day was just to see new people, meet new faculties, and swear upon new friendships destined to last life times and love affairs bound to make bad poets of boys and agony aunts of girls. There was no ragging as such, most boys were busy marking their territories and eyeing potential mates, demonstrating machismo like guerillas, howling like wolves and growling at those who they perceived as a threat to the image they were trying to project. The girls came dressed in their best clothes, color that spoke out loudly that they are available, the already committed ones, who mostly belonged to the city, had either decided to skip the day completely or were standing near the parking lot talking to their boyfriends, whether those lucky boys belonged or did not belong to the college nobody knew or cared. The management was relaxed, the target had been met or most probably exceeded, and all those road trips by the staff to remote villages to coax kids and parents into admissions through fake talent tests had been fruitful. If one observed keenly he would be able to spot traits of the famous movie stars, the tight t-shirts, temporary tattoos, hair colors, accessories, boisterous laughs and feminine awwws, everything was at display.

A month had passed since the sessions began, the first week had seen classrooms brimming with students, admissions were still coming in but once the students settled and understood that there was no point coming to college regularly, the attendance started dwindling and in the end only two kinds of students ended up frequenting college on non examination days, the first were those who strongly believed in the institution of formal education and really wanted to learn believing in a bright, corporate future, these were very few, and the second were the ones who wanted a safe place to sit and discuss with their girlfriends without being spotted by their guardians or somebody who knew them, it was too early to fret about a stable job. Karan belonged to neither of the two categories but he still went to college because he didn't know what else to do all day, his dad had not bought him a bike to enable his free movement in the city, the bus dropped him to college and picked him up in the evening. Everything that a boy needs to survive could be found around him, a barber shop where he could sit and watch television and a general store to buy meal replacements in the form of potato chips and coke. Dad had come for a day and brought him home made food and some money that he may need, it was not much and much below city's rate card but he didn't know that, this was his first time and he was also learning. Lazy and non-committal like he was, Karan also didn't ask his father for more money. The bank account had not been opened yet so he put all the extra money inside his pillow cover, the chain gave him a sense of security that no one would take it. The money was largely safe and unspent, not because he was frugal with it but because he had not discovered avenues of spending it yet, truth be told, he still hadn't discovered his spending patterns, this was the first time in his life that he was the in charge of keeping and spending money from a limited allotted pool.

CHAPTER 4

ADAPTATION

The first year had gone by like a breeze, the exams were over and results were awaited. Karan was back home for a good whole month, at home he was still the same if not sloppier in the hygiene and cleanliness department but outside he was an all new boy. He had grown his hair at the back, like an American mullet, he wore colorful t-shirts with messages that said things like 'My Dad is an ATM'. Mr. Surana did not like this changed look of his son, especially the t-shirt with that message. He fumed in private and confided in his wife, asking her to convince her son about being a gentleman and not look like a goon from across the railway line. His language had changed considerably, the use of mispronounced English words had gone up to a point that an English knowing gentleman would think he is speaking some local Indian language. But there were no proper English speaking people in the suburb and he came across as an uber urban dude to a lot of locals. As a result his name started popping up in conversations amongst girls, they would watch him whenever he crossed and he brushed them off propagating a yarn that he hung out with girls ten times sexier than these and didn't really think much of this local produce. There were other changes too that his mother took as signs of growing up, secrecy with his cell phone, new bunch of friends, asking for more money and loud ring tones. Thirty days passed and he was more excited to go back than ever. With the help of mom he had convinced his dad to get him a 125 CC bike, better than nothing, there were two conditions though, one: to swear on his mother that he will always wear a helmet and not ride fast and two: to never have girls as pillion, no matter how needy they may be.

Within two months of the second year, Karan's attendance had dropped to nil, his girlfriend had still not returned from her hometown and there was no real incentive to attend lectures that did not interest him anyways; he had not developed an affinity for any stream, from the popular lore that goes on in colleges, he knew that those who opt for finance get jobs with high salaries, more girls go for HR and those who struggle badly end up taking marketing and getting jobs as salesmen or only get hired by call centers.

Yash had not gone home for vacations and had decided to stay back in the city on the pretext of a project. On his return, Karan found few other guys sleeping in the house. There were beer bottles everywhere and empty packs of cigarettes thrown on the floor like a piece of décor. Yash saw him open the door using his key, looked at him with half shut eyes, told him the guys will be gone in an hour or so and slept again. The guys had been frequenting the room pretty often; they were the kinds Karan's dad had warned him against. They smoked, drank, had girl friends, used foul words in every sentence and spent a lot. He didn't like them all that much but to fit in, he would smoke a cigarette or two and drink a bottle of warm beer just so that they didn't think of him as some momma's boy. He would have drank more but was worried that in case some day these guys asked him to buy them booze in return of all the beer that he had had, he won't be in a position to refuse and where will he get the money to treat them, and if he ran out of money, how will he ask dad for more without giving a proper reason, he couldn't just make things up after all, and what if he became an alcoholic and died like that hero in the movie. What a shame!

Karan's girlfriend, Shivani, arrived the next week, he went to receive her on his bike with a Dairy Milk and a flower, he couldn't afford anymore, and anyway it is the thought that counts. It was time to resume college; he bought some new t-shirts and a pair of shades from one of the various knock-off shops on the sidewalks. Helmet had already been used up as an ashtray at the flat and thus both the promises made to dad were broken, but what else are the promises for. His expenses had gone up considerably, weekend visit to the mall, a movie on Friday, some dinner at affordable eateries, mobile phone recharges and petrol hovering around 80 a liter made sure that he used more money in three months than he had in the entire first year. Mr. Surana warned him about the ills of overspending and lectured him about his hair and clothes and text messaging but still increased his allowance after much reluctance.

Yash didn't go much to college either but he was rarely at the apartment, one of his friends was the son of a local politician and Yash had decided to be a part of his group. College elections, Strikes, *Dharna*, Assembly activity or any other politically motivated exercise and you would find him out with other party members, soon he had created a big set of friends and his phone used to ring constantly for discussions that Karan didn't really understand. In contrast, Karan had a very few friends, his girlfriend took up most of his time and most of her friends were his friends too, he was a part of this unsaid group of couples where you would be talked to only if you had a girlfriend. He didn't really care about friends, he had some back in school who he met whenever in town but otherwise it was only bulk texting of jokes that constituted his interactions. He spent most of his time on the internet, liking pages, and stalking his girlfriend. He had met Shivani during one of those college sponsored activities and found her easy to talk to. He didn't really love her till one day, inspired by some movie he decided that he had to have a girlfriend, it was an absolutely must to climb the social ladder; without a girlfriend he would never get entry in those exclusive couples only parties that take place in big hotels. How depressing would it be to go to a mall where all the boys come with their partner and he would go alone with his mini me in his hand. Keeping all these practical issues in mind and with a little help of beer and some encouragement from Yash and his friends, he dropped her a message at midnight. No reply came, which was a relief, she must have fallen asleep he thought. Next day, when the beer induced bravery subsided and he realized what could go wrong he decided to skip college, he skipped the first two lectures but the suspense was just too much to take, the nervousness made him feel like throwing up. He hadn't received a message still; she couldn't be sleeping for so long! By noon he got a message from Shivani's friend asking where he was and Shivani was looking for him. The guilt was too much to take; he bathed and left for college.

It was better to be yelled at once than die in anticipation, he couldn't avoid her forever, his best bet was that the message delivery had failed due to some network error and she didn't get any message after all.

The cat and mouse game went on for a week, Shivani had received the message but being a girl she had not found it exciting enough and was sure it was a case of drunken texting. Finally after a lot of ignoring and psychological warfare she succeeded in making him ejaculate an admission of his feelings for her, this led to a candle light dinner which he clearly couldn't afford but had to ritualistically get done with, but that is as far as it went, Shivani lived in a hostel and Karan was not too 'forward' himself, he was straight and all that but it was just the first date and nailing her would be a little too ambitious.

———◆•◆•◆———

CHAPTER 5

LET THE GAMES BEGIN

Second year was drawing to a close but it was still a while before the vacations. Karan had run out of all the money his dad had sent him, he had borrowed some money from friends and some from Yash but had squandered all of it. Now the friends were asking for it, for a while he worked on borrowing money from one friend to pay the other but even he knew that this won't last forever. He was in debt of Rs. 10,000 with no source of income in sight. His father had already refused to give him a single rupee till the end of the year; he had overdrawn on dad's generosity and could not ask him again.

There was television in the apartment now, popular T20 matches were round the corner and with one of the few places with television and no supervision, and a lot of guys were planning to watch the matches at his place. On the opening day of the league, there were just four of them at home. Yash, two of his friends whom Karan had not met earlier, all the three were carrying 2 phones, even Yash, a phone that Karan had not seen earlier. "When did you get this phone?" Karan asked. "Today", replied Yash casually, the games are beginning today so had to get a SIM card in somebody else's name and the three friends laughed sharing some inside joke. Karan did not get it but decided to not pursue it any further. It took a while, but he caught on pretty soon, the guys were betting, all three of them. There was a person on the other line who was declaring odds when asked and the three boys were placing bets with their pseudonyms. This was all very new for Karan; he had heard of betting but had never seen it in person. The match ended and some celebrations were in order, all three of them had won Rs.20,000 a piece. How easy is that! Karan thought to himself, the things they betted on even he could have guessed and here he was losing sleep over the money he owed those cheapskates; he could just play a few games, win the money and pay all the guys five times over, bloody beggars!

The bookie network in the city entertained only old customers and their references; with match-fixing allegations becoming big news the police had become more stringent but not too much, there was just enough wiggle room for the book makers to either escape without leaving any trace or get away with just a slap on the wrist. The experienced betters used SIM cards registered in other's names or with false details while the handsets were cheap and dispensable at the whiff of a threat. He had seen in the movies that no matter how much money a man illegally makes, he dies a dog's death while the honest ones go on to live a good, fulfilling life, kids and all. But the need of money was such that he decided to not pay attention to the adages and do what is best for survival; after all, what good is goodness that leaves you wretched and relying on generosity of others?

———◆•◆•◆———

It had all been worked out, after almost pleading Yash to refer him to a bookie; Karan was ready to bet in his first match. Yash had gotten him a credit of 10,000 to start with and had not really asked him for anything in return, Karan thanked him profusely and bought him two pints of his favorite beer and a pack of cigarettes, and he knew that if everything works out fine, he will pay Yash back in no time. It was the day of the MI v/s RR match, Karan was nervous and excited, his pituitary was releasing endorphins, he was high, and was sure his heart was doing at least a hundred beats a minute, the blood rushing to his head making him feel dizzy, he had messaged his girlfriend that he isn't well and would be sleeping the day off. There was a week old beer kept in the refrigerator that was used more as a cupboard for keeping things, it had stopped functioning a while ago but nobody cared, after all if you had a choice of getting either the television or the fridge repaired, you will choose the television hands down. He decided to drink it up, without worrying about the taste before the guys came back to watch the match, he didn't want to look too eager, too nervous or too scared, he already felt these three things, but there is a difference between feeling and showing.

The match began with a round of cigarettes and a packet of chips, there were various options to bet, predicting the number of runs a team will make in certain overs, the final total or the end result of the match. Karan realized how easy prediction was when there was no money to lose, but suddenly the same thing was full of uncertainty, he was scared of losing money, it wasn't as easy as it looked to the outsider, either he could blindly guess or he could go by his experience of watching different players on TV playing for their respective national teams, would the toss play a role? Was the pitch conducive for hitting in the later overs? Will the ball turn enough to restrict the batsmen? These were some of the questions he had never thought of till today and now he was not sure, anything can happen, it was a game. What if he loses all the money? The guys will think he is a fool, and then he will be under more debt. "Want to bet on the final score?" His train of thought was derailed by Yash's nudge. "Do you think the final score would be below or above 180?" "I don't know, what if I lose? What do you think?" Yash snickered, "We think that with Watson still playing, they will cross, but it's your money man, you can sit out if you want to or make money, your call". The others seemed to be looking at him, judging him, thinking what a wuss he is. They will go out and tell their friends about this chicken of a boy. He couldn't let that happen. "Yes, I think they will go above 180". With a pat on the back, Karan called up the bookie and registered the bet, not for much, only for 2000. The bets were low and the team easily crossed the 180 mark. He had won 800 rupees, this was the first time he had ever won anything; in his life he had never found even a ten rupee note on the ground and here he was winning money worth 8 beers.

He put safe bets the entire night and ended up with a profit of 1750 rupees. "When will I get the money?" With a lot of trepidation he decided to accompany Yash to the bookie's lair. It was on the outskirts of the city, in a pretty rundown colony he never knew existed. They parked the bike at a distance and began walking.

CHAPTER 6

GETTING TO KNOW THE BIG GUYS

All the walk-ins were instructed to come in after dusk and leave before dawn for obvious reasons. The place was dank; one could smell urine on the walls and pigs snorting at some distance. Karan was wary of stepping into a pile of fresh shit, ruining his brand new sneakers which he had purchased recently. The betting had paid off better than he had expected, he played safe and made enough to pay off debts of those he wanted to pay and told the rest that he doesn't have the money and to not pester him further, he will return the dues once dad sends him something. He had bought a dual SIM phone for Shivani and for himself, some new t-shirts and these pair of shoes that weren't new anymore.

The bookie's den was not how he had expected to be, nobody wore suits or smoked cigars, there were no bulky sidekicks wearing netted vests and giving mean looks without reason. They were a bunch of men, the ones you would not notice if they crossed you by, some wore shirts, some t-shirts and denims, they were drinking tea and could have been just a bunch of friends sitting there doing nothing but for a wall with a switch board, that you could have found in legitimate BSNL exchanges, to which over 50 phones were miraculously connected. The day they first went to the place, the men were busy counting money and making complex entries in the notebooks, Karan didn't know about Yash but he had never seen so much money together at one place in his life. Some men there acknowledged Yash making it clear that he had been there before; he introduced Karan with his phone name, Yuvi, named after the player. There was no small talk; the air was heavy with seriousness of illegal activities. In a yellow polythene bag which they got from a local bakery, they put in their 1,00,000 rupees, bowed to everybody in general and quickly retreated. Of the one Lac, eighty belonged to Yash and his friends and twenty belonged to Karan.

———◆◆◆———

Things were different now, Karan Surana was no more a dull guy in the eyes of a common student, he knew the bullies of college and made it a point to chat up with them whenever he got a chance in full view of as many students as he could time at the moment. His clothes had become brighter and his attendance had dropped to an all time low of 5% in the entire last semester.

Initially when he had begun attending college, exams threatened him, the fear of failure made him give up on his love for sleep and he studied to at least have a shot at clearing the examination in the revaluation. But after a few exams he understood that he needn't waste time in going through the books. All he needed was to go through question papers of last three years and he was good to get over 60%. He knew that as long as he got that 'first class' he would be achieving more than anybody expected of him and his parents won't mind, and he was right, if the end is desirable, the means are not important.

College elections were about to begin, national political parties were working hard to get the member of their respective youth wings win the elections across various colleges and create a student body. Before now, Karan always wondered why these serious politicians who sit in the assembly interfered so much with student elections which meant nothing but now he understood that the quest for power has to take roots from the very beginning, the bigger the youth base the better the chances of creating a wave and winning the all important elections that matter. The more the number of goons the better are the chances of terrorizing locals and capturing polling booths to win the elections.

Yash had become an all out student leader and was contesting elections from his college, every day at the apartment his friends would come down discussing strategies but mostly bragging about how they were able to bribe or threaten professors into making sure that their group members won and how the students were told that though the voting would be done secretly, they will find out who voted for whom and destiny for the voters will take its course accordingly. Poor voters, just like their parents, the middle class, powerless and penny-less citizens had two choices, either to side with one of the two parties of gangsters or to keep their heads down and listen to and bear whatever was meted out to them. This time Karan had taken the former route, he was a member of the election management team of one of the students named Shatru Yadav. Shatrughn, popularly known as Shatru was a friend of Yash, his father was a farmer and a former MLA; this had given him a head start into the world of politics. Since his days of schooling, Shatru believed in moving around in numbers. Be it going to school or to a party, he always had at least 6 people accompanying him. The people created a kind of safety net for Shatru, they would praise him, fight on his behalf and intimidate others with his name, and in return they never had to pay for food, drinks or commute. The trend continued in college, whenever Shatru arrived, which was rare and had nothing to do with education, he came in an open gypsy carrying his 'friends'. They usually showed up during college fests or weekends, on the days they could flash their assets to girls, the primal behavior was at full display in all its glory, the powerful male peacocking his strengths, trying to attract the female, ever ready to fight with another male who could pose a threat. The territorial behavior went to the extent of parking the vehicle where they wished, and in the process destroying vehicles and egos of weaker males. The groupies shared a symbiotic relation as the one shared by Remora and Sharks and not a parasitic relation of animals and leeches. Both the parties milked and got milked readily to fulfill their ambitions and meet their goals. Karan had also jumped on the gypsy; all he wanted was to be identified with the big guys of the city who could lend him an identity and money when needed. Attending their parties and posting photos as a proof made him feel good. Telling people that he knew Shatru or Yash and they had just sat together last night discussing various issues made him feel important. Not blessed with a personality to intimidate or browbeat students, his job was to help others abduct those who were the contenders for the student body position. Being in the final year and more regular to college than the rest of them, he knew most of the contestants by face, whenever the boys stepped out of college or went to a nearby *chai ki dukaan*, he would call up the members who would be invariably parked nearby and let them know who it is that they need to pick. It was easy, the guys who got kidnapped for a day didn't know who gave them away and his name never came up.

Later on the university claimed that the elections were only a formality and the real power lay in the hands of the management; disregarding the number of withdrawals of nomination, missing students and injured candidates, the papers termed the elections as peaceful and a success. Shatru had won the elections and with a lot of effort had become the student body president; winning elections was easy but to become the president was not because in the end at least one of the parents of all those who won were rich and powerful and held enough clout to alter decisions. The professors usually turned the other eye towards the law and order situation whenever it arose in colleges; they were not paid well enough to stand up against their students who had the potential to publically humiliate them. They knew well enough that they may be able to fake dominance inside the campus, but once they'd step out of those iron gates it was a level playing field, more skewed against the working class which had everything to lose in case of a conflict. Moreover, it was better to befriend such guys and get more students to their privately run tuitions that ran so well that the salaries from college seemed meager in front of all the envelopes they got at the end of the month, tax free.

———◆•◆•◆———

Chapter 7

Missing the Train

Colleges are microcosm of society, it takes few of all kinds to complete the college experience, depending on the choice of college, one finds attention seekers, love birds, *netas*, goons, depressed, shy, loud, indifferent and career focused; this college had its serious students as well, so in the final semester when students were busy preparing for CAT because apparently that is what any serious student must aspire to do, get into an IIM, or those a little less delusional were filling forms to get into some famous private college, Karan was busy associating himself with people of questionable repute just so that he can gain some kind of fame he hoped will help him in the future somehow. Just like the entrance exams before choosing this college, he filled the form for some colleges for the heck of it and also because his girlfriend, who like most girls was a more worthy student than him, had advised him to do so. After a lot of negotiations he had convinced his dad that he will have to go to Pune to fill in some forms and that he will go alone with his friends, conveniently omitting that the primary reason of this academic tour was to accompany his girlfriend.

Money was not a problem at the moment, with all the winnings from the matches he had paid off all the creditors and had some money left to make the trip, his father had given him some extra money for the trip, Shivani also carried some money with her so financially the trip was viable. Travelling in a general sleeper compartment and eating at corner shops would save them enough money to splurge at some club on the last night. Being in a town, they had never been to a real club, the kinds they show on the tele. Their usual hangouts were pubs and restaurants which somehow felt inferior to those establishments in the city which are frequented by celebrities and cricket stars. He had googled some places, out of which they will visit one on the trip.

———◆•◆•◆———

It was an overnight journey and Karan was travelling with 3 other colleagues, one being his girlfriend, a friend of his girlfriend and the boyfriend of that friend of his girlfriend. The journey began with a lot of excitement, this was his first trip of the kind, the camaraderie of the four was similar to the one shared by those who partner up in a crime. The guys would alight on every small station depicting some kind of machismo, the girls would gawk and gush and squeal asking them to get back on the train, and how they will face the city if their knights got left behind! The hi-fives, the nudges, the jokes and the winks died down as the experience started losing its luster. The guys were carrying some cheap vodka that they had mixed in a bottle of Thumsup, thus adding an extra thrill to their journey. As the night descended and the sounds in the bogey died down, the couples sat next to each other, holding hands, whispering. The lights were shut and only faint silhouettes were visible through the common bulbs in the aisle that would be on all night. Karan was intently listening to some childhood memory of Shivani but his attention was partially fixed on the couple that sat across them on the side berth. The guy was clearly trying to kiss the girl, starting with her hands on the pretext of some emotionally drenched line that he had come up with. Karan watched with interest, he was never that kind of a guy, dating Shivani was more the result of him being encouraged to do so, but now that he was into it he wanted to go all the way and add another story to his life. While he was still thinking about it, the two co-passengers quietly got up and left towards the door of the car. Shivani also noticed but said nothing, taking a cue from her, Karan also curbed his initial thought of following them;

he was sure that with everybody sleeping around they were making their way to the washroom for some action. He had noticed the straying eyes of the boy and with his new friends back at college he knew what his intentions were.

They reached the city early morning and decided to lodge in a cheap hotel close to the college. It was only a day's trip, the girls seemed sincere in filling the forms while the boys decided to take a tour of the campus and compare girls of the city to those at home. The girls there were clearly hotter, wore shorter clothes and used English more frequently than their girlfriends; Karan's makeshift friend tried some small town trick to get a girl's attention but after failing, he just labeled city girls as desperate whores who want money and decided to stay satisfied with what he had. The girls had filled application forms on behalf of their boyfriends too, hoping to carve out a long term love story while the boys stood near the canteen and smoked.

Over the years, Karan's alcohol intake had gone up and cigarette consumption was only curbed due to lack of money; he had heard a lot about how city folks were more into sophisticated drugs like hash, marijuana, LSD and the likes but he had no clue as to which one of them were eaten, smoked, snorted or injected. He had heard stories of film stars doing cocaine and was sure that it must be a great high if the rich ones were doing it.

It had been a week since they got back from the trip. Last night at the club was a blur for Karan, he had finally scored a joint and smoked it furiously, coupled with the drinks and the people around, he had soon lost track of time and actions. He remembered doing a couple of shots, then smooching Shivani while feeling her up, she had resisted initially but when she saw that nobody around bothered, she had let him do it. After couple more drags in the washroom and a shot of Kamikaze he had no recollection of the events of the night. He does not remember that he had thrown up on the dance floor and the bouncers had escorted him out, Shivani was with him but the other two people were missing. Either they did not know about him or had decided to ignore him and stick to the plan; he had paid for the drinks and the table already. He had fallen asleep in the rickshaw on the way to the bus stand and lay knocked out on the pavement for at least half an hour before his body felt thirsty and dehydrated and insisted him to get up and have some water.

The bus departed at 8 and the other two friends showed up at 7 pinning the blame on Karan for ducking out of the party without informing and how they searched for him but after a while decided to stay back as they had nowhere else to go. Everybody looked wasted but Karan was the worst of the lot. His head throbbed and he tried to sleep as soon as he got into the bus. Other than some small talk, Shivani did not talk to him and he was in no condition to notice or ask her about it.

Shivani was mad at him about something but he didn't know what it was. He was sure it had to do with that last night but was too scared to ask her, for all he knew, he could have hit on some girl other than his girlfriend or treated her inappropriately. In any case he decided to generically apologize for anything that he may have done wrong. Shivani had seen a very different side of Karan that night, the usually shy and quiet boy who occasionally hung out with the wrong kind of guys but didn't indulge in unlawful acts was loud and abusive that night. He had tried to forcefully put his hand up her dress, when denied he had pushed her and walked off, she could clearly see him looking at other girls and trying to dance with them on the floor before he threw up. It had been a few years and the novelty of the relationship had clearly worn off, but after that night and with their academic life coming to an end, Shivani had decided to break up with Karan, it was easier to end it with a guy who was not really going anywhere in life than to defend your choice in front of the displeased parents.

CHAPTER 8

THE REHAB

His bachelors had come to an end, the exams were over, he was pretty sure that he will not have to appear in any re-exams for any of the subjects and even if it ever came to that, now he knew enough people in the university who would be glad to help in return of some money.

After the final semester got over, Karan wanted to live in the city but with father's pestering and depleting cash reserves the best bet was to go back home and rest a little. The ambitious ones were busy visiting colleges for higher education or working at entry level positions. Karan had no interest in studying further; neither did his parents want him to waste more of their money and his time in getting another useless degree by crawling through the syllabus. They were just hoping that with a degree in his hand he will be able to land himself a job that will in turn enable them to find a decent girl for him.

Since he had returned home, Karan had done nothing much in the name of job hunting. He watched television

54

all day or was busy texting people, networking, he called it; Mr. Surana had indirectly displayed his displeasure at his son's lack of application but the news of kids committing suicide because the parents won't leave them alone made him implode without letting the shards of his anger reach his son.

To appease his mother, Karan kept on talking about some big business that he planned to set up, if only his father had more money just like that of his friends. When his mom forced him about divulging his master plan, he mentioned that he wanted to start a restaurant as hospitality business had a good ROI; he didn't know if this was true but he had just used some heavy terms that he had learnt at college to convince his mother of his ability and vision.

The day he had met his friends for tea, he discussed the restaurant idea with them, not knowing much about the business, they only shared anecdotes and examples that had been passed to them from somebody else who did not know much about the business but knew enough to share some stories that sounded very wise but if you reflected upon them, there was very little to take away.

Karan did not know about the business either, he just wanted to open a bar, which he had mentioned as restaurant to save an argument with his parents, because he believed there was a lot of money in it. He didn't have any real plan but was sure that the network of friends that he had created in the city will help him get a place and also keep the bad guys off his property. When he had shared this plan with Yash, he thought that his roommate had a look of approval and he was promised full support and cooperation in any way that he needed.

————◆•◆•◆————

Home comfort was something that did not take time in getting used to. With the plan stored in a shelf somewhere and his parents not pestering him anymore, Karan settled down at home, satisfied with what he got without working for it. Drinking and smoking had become difficult, yes but he did not have to worry about arranging some money or borrowing it from anybody for the time being and that made him happy. Sometimes, on the pretext of somebody's birthday, he would borrow some cash from his dad and go to the farthest bar possible to down a couple of drinks. He missed the matches though; the high that he got from betting was missing. He had gotten a call from Inzamam the other day, this was the name of the bookie he used to place his bets with, he was pretty sure that the name was made up but he didn't really care. Of the 3 years he spent in the city, nothing gave him more satisfaction than winning big money at the games. The biggest he had won in a day was 30,000 and it was then that he got hooked. Up till then, his bets were smaller and reluctant, the amount of money he used to win earlier was disproportionately less to the fear his heart felt, then one day he got drunk and kept raising his bets on both the games as suggested by his friends and by his standards he hit Gold. It all seemed to be over now, there was no way his father could cough up any more money, and there was no kind of paternal or maternal property. Nobody would lend him money, stupid he may be but with the various experiences he had understood that people don't mean what they say. So it was pretty much on him. He didn't have any excuses left, he was not a kid anymore waiting for his dad to get him admitted, sadly, he was not unqualified anymore. Well fuck it, his mind gave a signature response; he was already in an unpaid rehab with good food, cable and steady cash when needed. There was still time to hang around, refresh his mind from the toil of past two decades and plan ahead, something will come up sooner or later, maybe a job requirement in dad's factory, he had a degree after all, better, he might get some funding, miracles happen with people, they don't become rich just by hard work, they propagate such tall deeds so that others get disheartened even before trying and the rich remain those few storytellers banking money in their family.

CHAPTER 9

BEING EMPLOYED

The first day at work was the polar opposite of the first day at college. The day he walked into the office nobody turned to look at him, some people glanced but dismissed him as just another guy in the office. He was supposed to report to the manager, the man who had taken his interview, Mr. Nayar, or just Nayar Sir. It is not that Karan had bloomed into a professional since he left college, it just so happened that he had half heartedly registered with an employment agency and they had called up informing him about a job opening in the city. The job seemed pretty simple, all he had to do was get leads from the internet and some database that had more wrong entries than the right ones, make calls, drop mails or walk on hands, do anything humanly possible to meet the concerned person and pitch his company's services.

On the day of his scheduled interview, only a few guys had walked in, most of them looked older or academically less qualified than him. Karan couldn't care less about the reason; all he cared about was that of the 8 applicants, he was selected. He was sure it was his communication skills and confidence and there was no way to find out. He was in; the starting salary was 12,000 plus travel allowance and incentives if you met your sales goals every quarter. He didn't tax his mind too much about calculating the bonus percentage, with the job he was achieving quite a few things, a much craved silence of his dad, money and a chance to move back to the city. He informed all the friends that he was moving back and had a job. The college days of carelessness and debauchery were still green in his head. It was time to be the man his father never thought he would become.

———◆•◆•———

Nobody gave a fuck about anybody at work. It had only been over a month at work but felt like a decade or so. Well, even if he exaggerated he was amazed thinking about the longevity of Mr. Surana at his workplace. From his first job till his retirement in five years, how did he manage it? How could he get up every morning and slide under the sheets every night without fail, to do the same job with same kind of sincerity over and over every day. How could he not fall ill despite not being a proponent of fitness by any length, and even when he did catch flu it did not last for more than two days or only fell during a weekend.

The city was hot and going to nearby industrial zones pitching some kind of a shitty internet plan to those already using better but expensive ones sounded like a great idea in the first couple of weeks but not anymore. All his delusions of being charismatic, and a driven marketing genius were shattered by wrong numbers, bouncing mails and abusive listeners. He still hadn't converted any lead of the seven you needed to convert in a quarter to gain hefty bonus, but sure had a few good starts to talk about, sales people will tell you how getting a foot in the door is important, just make sure to not get your dick caught in it. But he was not going to give up this job; he knew he was lucky to get it, the money was ok to begin with, much more than he ever thought he would get and they told him that entry level positions only fetch half of his salary even in the most reputed of firms. Not that he will not try and convert a lead, why wouldn't he but not right now, it was too hot and it was time to go home and sleep on the pretext of a sales call.

Yash wasn't home, as usual, he had texted Karan saying he won't be back for the night so that he may instruct the maid to not cook a meal for him. It hadn't been hard for Karan to start his life from where he had left it; Yash had failed in a few subjects and had another semester to go so he was still living in the same apartment, Karan decided to move in the same house again; he didn't like too much change anyway. To the chagrin of his dad, he told him that it is a temporary arrangement and that he will move out when he gets a better and cheaper place to stay. Out of boredom and the itch to reclaim his relationship status and also because he could not find anybody else, Karan had used all the tricks in the book to emotionally weaken Shivani to get back with him. She was now pursuing Masters while working as an intern at the same college, counseling students and filling seats. It had taken quite a few dry sobs, the threat to go alcoholic and to kill himself to win her over; with Yash gone, Karan had called her over to the house, with the maids given an off, the house was all to himself. She left office at 7 and her hostel gates were shut at 9 so they had a couple of hours to themselves, enough to do what grownups do. Things were different though, unlike college, office couldn't be bunked as per convenience. Even if you half heartedly worked or intentionally slacked the grueling hours took their toll on a boy who hadn't really worked at all for the first quarter of his life, assuming he will die at eighty.

As the time passed Karan became more annoyed with himself and his life. The job for him had been an escape route from his dreary town life, but he hadn't been as free as he thought he would be. Slacking and missing targets got him in the eye of Mr. Nayar who was not a man to mess with. He did not call anybody in the room, whatever had to be said, the threats, the appreciation happened on the office floor where all the seventy people, including the office boys, could listen and decide who is to be respected and gotten tea and who must be ignored knowing that he can't demand the privileges of the office and can't do much about it. His whereabouts were closely monitored; after all he couldn't be taking an afternoon power nap at home on company's payroll. Because of employees like him, Mr. Nayar had created a new policy where all the sales team must fill out a sheet every Saturday stating the names of the offices they had scheduled the meetings with next week and these were reviewed every Monday from 10 to noon. This not only forced the sales people to fix meetings so that their sheets looked populated, but also visits or at least call the offices they had listed in the previous week; as a result Karan lost all the empathy of his colleagues who had been doing similar things but were sure that they would get away by doing the same at least for another year if not for Karan who skipped going to a fixed meeting and the fuming manager whom he was supposed to meet called up on the office landline yelling about the failure of the office's sales representative to turn up at the meeting on time thus wasting his entire day. This call was transferred to Mr. Nayar who had apologized profusely for the slip up and later made sure that the entire floor knew he does not want *haraamkhors* like Karan to be in his company anymore, of course he had not fired him but he had set an example of him by deducting his salary of two days and introducing the sales forecast procedure which put every outbound employee in a lurch.

Being employed was not a good thing, he was surprised how his dad had lasted so long, he couldn't work anymore but had to find another way to make money before he could spit on Mr. Nayar's face and throw the resignation letter on his table.

Chapter 10

Inzamam & Company

He wanted to be a cricketer; all the fandom of the *mohalla* where he was the most feared batsman gave him the confidence that soon he will play state and then national. But there was not enough money to attend the selection camps and get noticed by anybody who mattered. Moreover there was no IPL in those days, and then he would surely have been one of the highly valued players on the roster. But it was all gone, he had crossed 50 last week and Shaqib was associated with Cricket not as a player but as a bookie, he went by the name of the favorite batsman, Inzamam, also because he was equally overweight and had problem speaking English. He was not well educated but knew the ins and outs of cricket better than anybody else. He knew the fielding placements, could predict the possible moves of the captain and could read the pitch by looking at the past stats and television coverage. The rates and the odds were forwarded from Mumbai and it was Inzamam's role to pass it on to the local callers, collect money or disburse it as the fate might be. He did his own little betting by the side to make some extra money over the percentage. He had been in the business for the past twenty years and had seen the ups and downs of the game and of the people who placed their incomes, lives and hopes over the 22 yard pitch. He knew of people who had become millionaires through betting, but those were few and the ones who already had some kind of back up, both financial and political, but more than that were the kinds who lost everything and spent rest of their lives in a state of paranoia, running away from the men who just wanted their money. These losers were usually the novices who had entered the ring desperate but who could not step out without finishing the game. In the past few years, the lure of money and good life had brought in various youngsters. Most of them placed small bets and were a pain in the ass; they didn't understand the jargon and pestered him a lot. But these boys were the ones who got him more money and more people. They lost more than they won and whenever they won they placed bigger bets, eventually losing all the money. Then they would go quiet for a few months, returning with a vengeance to win the lost money and continued the cycle further.

Not wanting to involve Yash anymore and also because he didn't meet him much, Karan had decided to contact Inzamam, he wanted to be very rich, he wanted to show Mr. Nayar and the likes that he didn't give a fuck about such jobs and he keeps more money in his wallet than the entire month's salary which they could afford to give him, with bonus. With his past references and track record, he got his credit line up to 50,000. Inzamam also didn't mind honeytrapping him with an extended credit line, knowing full well that he may win some small hands but just one bad day and lapse of judgment and he would be extracting much more out of this new rat. Yash, who still maintained an account at Inzamam's center got to know about his roommate's re-entry into the market but didn't say anything about it, he knew that Karan will be the first one to tell him when the time is right.

He wasn't much of a cricket buff and knew only as much as an average fan would know, but the earlier streak that made him win more had given Karan a sense of confidence in his decision making and he did not think about consulting others for the bets he was going to make. Test was way beyond his capabilities and he could only guess with an amount of certainty in the shorter formats, more so when the contest was lopsided but the money he had won and the lack of guidance had given Karan a false sense of confidence and invincibility, he was sure that the decisions he took were well informed and that if he kept on continuing the streak, he would soon have enough money to be taken seriously by his friends. His whole life had been an exercise in gaining approval of others; right from the choice of text book stickers and other stationery in school to the kinds of clothes that he wore, girlfriend that he maintained and stories he delivered, every act was a way to gain more acceptance and acknowledgment. He couldn't tell why but he always felt inferior to others and to counter this feeling, the front he used to put up earlier was that of a withdrawn boy but the one he used now was that of a brash youngster with connections because he had seen this one work well for those others whom he followed.

Australia was going to play Sri Lanka down under and Karan could do with some extra money. The matches began earlier than his waking hours, but he had decided to tune in to the matches early morning and place bets. This was his first try at the non-T20 format and the first try in a match that was not between two clubs. He woke up and turned the television on; Yash was still asleep in his room not to be woken up by anything till noon. Karan lay in bed while watching Channel 9's commentary, he couldn't grasp it as easily as he could the Hindi one or for that matter the English one spoken by Indian commentators. Australia had won the toss and decided to bat, Karan knew only those players from both teams whom he had seen playing in the IPL. He had no real clue about the pitch, its history or the player profiles, except for the one they were showing on television. But gambling is a habit and sometimes you gamble without even knowing all the rules of the game. He was reluctant at first and decided to not watch the game and postpone betting for the next game. He switched the TV off and tried to sleep but the hormones had kicked in and he was excited. If he could bet on this game alone and win, he was sure he will earn some kind of a reputation amongst the friends. The game was on when he tuned in, he decided to bet on first 10 overs and predicted that the Aussies will cross the 80 run or above mark. They seemed to be cruising and had already made 70 for the loss of 1 wicket by the end of the 9th over. 2 boundaries and he will win 5000, just like that. The first ball was hit for a 4 and Karan was already planning his narrative. Second ball was a dot, only 6 runs more in 4 balls; the third ball swung out and narrowly missed both the batsman and the keeper sailing to the boundary in a quick outfield. How does it matter as long as he was getting runs? 78, Karan was just 2 runs and 3 balls away from his first international match money. He coolly gulped down some water from the bottle kept next to his bed. The 4th ball was played defensively for a run. Almost there, the joy was immense; he had made more money in the first 5 waking minutes of the day than some people do in a month. Then it happened, on the 5th ball, a slower one, the batsman miscued the hit making the ball stand up in the 30 yard circle, it was a soft dismissal, the players had crossed, giving the strike to the already set batsman. The hormones still had to settle, making Karan optimistic. He was just one run away from making money and was sure that the batsman will take a single to keep the strike in the next over. Pumped by the wicket, the next ball was a bouncer which the batsman ducked safely, Karan had lost.

It was as if he his bank had been robbed, he couldn't breathe and palms sweated, he couldn't watch the match anymore but neither could he look away. This is how it must feel to get punched hard in the stomach; the heart beat was touching the 100 mark. He just couldn't reason better. It was all gone; soon Inzamam's men will come after him. Will he ever see his parents again? Should he flee and head home? Change his name? "You are up early"! His train of thoughts was derailed by Yash who stood there in his pajamas and vest. "I woke up to the noise of TV, thought you must have left it on at night". Karan couldn't say anything. He just looked at Yash and blinked with a white face, remote held in a trembling hand. "Dude you look like someone just looted you at gunpoint".

Karan told Yash the entire story, barely restraining him from sobbing. It was only a loss of some 3000 odd rupees, that's ok, when you gamble, you win some, and you lose some. Yash told Karan that it was no big deal and he would be able to cover up in one good bet. Now Karan regretted not telling his friend about his plans. After a lot of convincing, Yash sat with Karan and supervised his bets for the ongoing game. By the end of it, they were better off with 4700 after recovering the lost 3500 of the bad bet. So in all they had made 8200 before the clock struck 12.

CHAPTER 11

NO FREE LUNCH

Since the morning of that first ODI, Karan had become indebted to Yash, not openly though. He had run through the balance sheet of his life and found out that it was only this guy, whom his dad hated, who had helped him the most number of times, both financially and psychologically, since he left home. He didn't know how will he ever pay this guy back, but one thing was certain, he will help him whenever the need may arise.

It didn't take long, the assembly elections were about to begin and Yash had been supporting the candidate nominated by the party from his ward. He needed people, a lot of people or volunteers to carry out things across the city. Putting up posters, distributing flyers, vandalizing the opponent's campaign, it was all in a day's work for a political henchman. Karan was taken to the party office, sitting in an open jeep with people who he had usually seen on hoardings or around college during the elections. Nobody spoke to him, he was used to it; they were busy talking amongst themselves about people he didn't know and events he hadn't seen. Like anything else in this whole wide world, he didn't know much about politics, and neither did he try to understand; he wasn't even sure who the current Prime Minister was, was it the guy with the turban, Khushwant Singh something or Gandhi's relative, he didn't have time for all this trivia. Soon they reached the office in the basement of a commercial building. There were a lot of people sitting on a formerly white bed sheet spread out on the floor. Their cumulative weight had thinned down the mattresses taken from some tent house. The footwear were scattered outside the door, not in their respective pairs anymore and the room stank of socks and unwashed feat. But nobody seemed to care, some were having tea and talking loudly about the elections, others were having tea and reading the evening news paper. Few workers were putting a bundle of flyers in order and giving one away to anybody who cared to take it. Karan didn't really care but he took it anyway, also pretending to read will help him avoid eye contact with people he didn't know, people who were much older or much knowledgeable or both. Yash put a hand on his shoulder and asked him to take a seat; he chose the farthest corner on the floor where a very old man sat with his back to the wall making some notes in his pocket diary. He sat next to him and immediately started scouring the flyer. It was printed in Hindi so that everybody could understand, the rulers of the country were not really educated enough to read and comprehend multiple languages, neither was he, Hindi will do just fine. The paper contained the symbol of the party on top, center aligned and a small, cropped picture of some leader on the top right corner. Below these were various bullet points talking about the developments the party had done and the incidences of corruption and mismanagement of the opposition. The format had a letter feel to it, as if the man on the bottom right is trying to address the reader personally. He got confused, of the two faces on the paper, which one was the candidate; he was answered by the sudden surge of activity in the room followed by loud sloganeering. The man who walked in looked similar to that pic on the bottom right corner of the paper he held in his hand; he was sure it's him, only for the complexion which was much darker in reality, thank you Photoshop. The man with bushy moustache and receding hair raised a hand and people hushed down, the guys who were distributing pamphlets till now brought a chair and a glass of water in the next 5 seconds. Few of the close associates went and stood behind the chair, one of them was Yash who stood quietly slightly towards the right hand of the leader, Sunder Sharma was his name, quite ironic, considering how he looked just the opposite. He whispered something in the ears of one of the older men standing in the group behind him, the man listened intently and then straightened up to speak, everybody's eyes were focused at him. He began his well rehearsed and often repeated speech. His voice was not as manly as his looks, but the confidence was evident, he had won the elections five years ago and the odds of reclaiming the seat were in his favor. In the past five years, he had assembled huge following, organizing popular festivals, giving free food, promising employment and harboring criminals; Yash had joined him through one of the recruitment drives and had gone up the ladder as one of his preferred men due to his network and ability to bring new people into the fold. Karan wasn't aware of this, even if he knew he wouldn't have cared, but he was one of the recruits.

———◆◆◆———

The first few tasks were easy, to go to a local printer and ask him to design and print flyers worth it didn't matter how much because politicians, no matter of what stature, are notorious for not paying in return of the products and services they choose to consume as long as they have the power, on the other hand no money can be expected of them if they lose the race. Other tasks included vandalizing hoarding sites and walls, putting up posters of Sunder

Sharma smiling and waving at his voters out on the roads. Usually the activities went on smoothly, followed by some booze and free food at restaurants owned by Sunder for whitening the election funds. But not all volunteers or workers were as privileged as those who were close to Yash or Sunder himself, others had to do with food cooked at home or whatever else they could find. Sometimes the things could take an ugly turn; on one of his assignments with four more men, Karan's group came across a group of nine men supporting the rival politician. Abuse and taunts ensued but things soon turned violent when the name calling went a little too far to the dislike of few of the already drunk men. The things were clearly not new for most of the guys and they soon took out knives and picked up stones readily available at the site. A brawl broke out and it was ugly, the guys lunged at each other with no real plan, most lost their knives and stones as they got excited and began using bare hands, one of the men from Karan's team got cornered and was being beaten by two guys, Karan stood frozen, clearly realizing that he was in no condition, physically or mentally, to intervene and save the guy, he just took out his phone and called Yash up, who luckily received his call after a few rings. In fifteen minutes, reinforcement arrived, in form of a police jeep, letting the guys know its arrival from over five hundred meters away with its blaring sirens. By the time it arrived the men from both the sides had run away leaving Karan and the severely injured worker. He could have run away too but the man lying there in front of him in a pool of his own blood and probably urine was the one on whose bike Karan had been riding as a pillion. Two heavyset, tanned and clearly weary men in *Khakee* uniforms got out of the vehicle. They looked at the lying body, checked him for breathing, looked at Karan with disinterest and asked him to get in the Jeep. "But what about..", he began but after noticing the look of the men decided to not pursue with his question, anyway the man was not his friend and reeked of sweat and cheap whisky. They drove for an hour, not to the police station, but to the party office. "Stay here, shut up and don't get out, else we will charge you with murder". That cold and crude statement was enough for Karan to shut his mouth and his brain. He sat there, shivering a little in thirty degrees while the policemen entered the office. They stayed there for about fifteen minutes which seemed like an hour; Karan's phone rang, he took it out of his denim pockets wet with nervous sweat, it was Yash.

Rizwan, that guy from the night was dead, it was in the evening papers, he didn't know him by name but recognized him from the blurred mugshot. The night before, Yash had called him to the office, asked him to get out of the jeep and leave for home on foot and there was no need to be worried about the police. He had obeyed like a scared lamb, once again indebted to Yash's clear orders and instructions in times of his indecision. But he knew it was not over, for the first time in his life he was not able to sleep well, wondering if he could have helped, but how? These questions kept him up and he knew well that now he had done possibly the first rarest thing of his life, witnessing a murder.

CHAPTER 12

IN TOO DEEP

He still had that job, but doing well and getting ahead was the last thing on his mind; he had bigger matters to think of and more money to make, but not the usual way. With his increasing involvement in local politics and the realization that there was money to be made without slogging at the office and belittling yourself, Karan's interest at work had diminished to a level where he just couldn't care less. But he cared just about enough to not lose his job, involvement with the party was not fetching him any real money just now, some losses in the matches made sure that he did not take up betting as his only job and a full time vocation was need of the hour to pay rents and manage other daily affairs. He had come up with a way of just about hanging on at his job; he made sure some people visited him frequently but not too frequently to drop in an indirect reminder about his connections. Normally it didn't really work in private organizations but this was a small city and the employees, at the end of the day, had to go back home on the streets that were ruled by people like Sunder Sharma.

An endomorphic frame, thanks to his inferior genes, Karan was never fit to play the part of a bully who got important things done for his master, like grabbing lands or solving a dispute via the last man standing method. He would have loved to be that guy everybody was scared of, loved to carry the mean face around on a bike doing whatever he wanted to do, no questions asked, but he just wasn't cut out for such tasks. He did try and work out in a local gym owned by one of those big guys who always wore sunglasses and tight t-shirts showing their huge arms and big stomach, he didn't even had to pay for the place, all of Sunder's men went there, it was like a barrack where phalanxes were trained to fight, but fee or no fee dedication had never been Karan's forte and his attendance at the gym slowly thinned down to permanent absence. He knew he didn't have to work that hard and spend all the money on supplements when he had already become popular at the party office. He was sure that people found him reliable and hard working; he did everything that Yash, who had now become the in charge of the youth wing, asked him to and the new boys who were regularly coming in took counsel from him and looked up to him.

It had been a while since that night, Yash had informed Karan that Rizwan was indeed dead and there was nothing he could have done to save him, had he tried, he would have died as well. The policemen were just playing their part and they were two of the many people Sunder had helped in getting a job. They had come there half hoping that Karan would be dead but he was not so to make things oblivious to the press they had dropped Karan back to the office. But to Karan it seemed like an incident that belonged to some distant past, he had graduated from being just a guy to increase numbers at a rally to being a serious worker who could resort to cruder practices if needed.

It happened one fine morning, he took off from the office at lunch and came to meet Yash at the party office, he had a couple of hours for a business meeting and decided to go out with men to a far off place and mediate a compromise between one of the guys who did some work on their behalf but was not a full time party worker and a local goon who had been stalking his girl friend and harassing her regularly. Both the men had had a heated conversation where the stalker had threatened him with serious consequences. The boy had helped Yash at one of the rallies earlier and had asked for help but with the laws strict and police on the lookout for people who can be made an example, Yash decided to skip the meeting and asked the men to settle the issue at a remote location. To make up for his last blip and prove that he had earned his place there, Karan got in with the guys.

The atmosphere was tense and heavy, the boy had joined them midway and the stalker had brought in three more men with him. Both the parties reached the rear of a dilapidated building to settle the scores. The meeting was being mediated and the men were asked to stay away from the girl in exchange of forgiveness but the four men on the other side of the table were not in the mood for any kind of arrangements, they told the men to mind their own business and leave the girl to them, for they would rape the girl anyway and the boy won't be able to do anything about it. This triggered it, the tension had been simmering and Karan knew that like most meetings of this kind, some bloodshed was inevitable. Summoning all the courage, and steadying his legs, he walked close to the boy from his right, their group outnumbered that of the would be rapists by one and this did the trick, the guys, obviously high on certain banned substances were so focused on Karan's gang that they did not notice the most harmless, unknown and till now a quiet guy of the group breaking to his right and moving closer to the men. In the high sounds of abuses, threats and counter threats, there was a muted sound of breaking glass and a loud yell. Soon everybody produced weapons, the finger punch, a chain, knives and in less than half a minute the battle was over. The stalkers, inebriated and slow to react, were badly injured. One had been hit on the nose releasing a fountain of blood and knocking him out instantly, the second was choked by two of them and had some fractured ribs, the third of the four had tried to run but had twisted his ankle badly, he just sat there and cried for mercy to no one in particular, the last guy, the real adversary lay there in his own pool of blood, other than the wound on his face which came from Karan breaking a bottle on it, the blood seemed to be steadily flowing out of his gut, the boy had found an opportunity and stab him twice while he lay on the ground unconscious from the mixture of drugs and loss of blood, it was certain that he would not rape anybody in his lifetime, good riddance.

———◆◆◆———

The news about the rendezvous spread fast and Karan could feel a change in the eyes of those who he was used to meeting every day. He perceived reverence and even fear on the faces of the lot, including the veterans. The young ones started greeting him more often and deliberately and he started getting tea with the important people. Sunder Sharma, who rarely talked to workers except for the important ones, tapped him on his back while talking to Yash and asked him if he was ok, he gladly nodded in affirmative. Acceptance! He was finally gaining it from people who really mattered.

The incident had instilled a kind of confidence that he never had, he walked broader and with more surety, his face had become sterner and voice firmer. Even those at the office had noticed it, and sometimes it seemed that they were aware of his recent feat. He decided to milk the perception of being a badass, his recently created band of followers, comprised of the office boys and security guards who are traditionally the first ones to get an in on what is happening in local politics. Karan now openly flouted office rules and felt invincible; Mr. Nayar who was the oppressor had now gone on the back foot, whether it was the news of his bravado or his body language he consciously began avoiding Karan in the corridors, growling and staring while he could, it sure pays to be with the right people.

CHAPTER 13

TIME

They were going to cut a 5 Kg cake today, celebrating 3rd anniversary of the company. Everybody was gathered for free cake and soft drinks, not to mention the *Samosas*. Karan was present as well, he did not want to be there, he wanted no affiliation with such a cheesy company where the idea of fun was cutting a cheap cake and letting the employees hog on some free food and winning a lifetime of loyalty in exchange But he was there, the elections were over and Sunder had won comfortably, so comfortably in fact that the opponent had left the venue midway through the counting, thus tacitly conceding defeat. Since then Yash, Karan and few others had risen up the ranks and Karan specially had learnt things he never thought he would. His language had changed to suit the roads, he could drink more and more often and violence didn't give him shivers anymore; he had learnt to cover his incompetence with muscle, of others.

Mr. Nayar had gone up the right rank to have the authority to cut the cake. People clapped, some looked eager to move on to the snacks table, Karan stood at the back, light on one leg, half leaning against the wall, his cheek was swollen and bruised, it had been like that for three days now, there was also a limp in his foot and he hobbled on a leg and half when he walked. He wanted to stay home and rest but since the elections and the lack of any matches that he could bet on, he had to work for salary, else the leave would have been an unpaid one. The injuries were from an altercation that had happened on the road a few days ago; while returning from a friend's place, he had banged into a family of 3 riding on a bicycle, the matter would have ended with an apology but the newfound realization of power and being untouchable made Karan get down and slap the man, engrossed in the act, he didn't expect a *chappal* that connected squarely and painfully with his face, it had come from the feisty wife who raised such a cry that in no time there were good 50 people standing in a circle, most of them were onlookers hunting for some excitement but few were those who enjoy beating people up in such commotion. The keys were taken out of his bike and thrown somewhere while two guys came behind him and launched a full fledged assault; had the traffic police not intervened Karan would definitely have blacked out in the next few seconds. People scattered while he lay there in a pile of shame, the family had left, he had not seen the assaulters to begin with so the anger building inside him was not directed towards anybody in particular. They could have been anyone, political rivals, opportunist onlookers, friends of that bicycle family. In the absence of the key, he dragged his bike to the side and began looking for the key, he didn't want to call anybody as that would let the story out, he took a bus, got a spare key from the house and rode the bike back. Such was the humiliation that he never wanted to come out of his room again, if people in the circle ever get to find out, he would lose whatever reputation he had created of himself. Yash had gone home for a few days, by the time he came back, the scars would be gone, and nobody needed to know. At the office he cooked up a story about a road accident for those who cared to notice.

Karan avoided going home, it had been a few months since he last visited, even if just for a day, Mr. Surana didn't complain, it was good that he didn't rely on them anymore, what else can a dad ask for, now all he had to do was find a suitable girl for his son. His mother didn't say much but she found her boy to be a changed man, he had gotten quieter than before and always looked somber, his lips looked blacker and he had an un-missable breath of a smoker. She tried asking him about his habits but he just dismissed the conversation off hand asking her to not worry about him as he was old enough to take care of himself. He didn't like staying at home anymore, the sheer pressure of hiding his habits and activities made the overall experience unappealing.

———————◆◆◆———————

There was a place, pretty close to Inzamam's headquarters that sold cheap grass, it was quite inferior to the one that was brought by guys from the hills but did the job for 100 rupees. A quarter of Royal Stag, a couple of cigarettes, a joint and he was all set to forget the pain and humiliation and go to sleep. In his dreams he would see things, a giant whose face resembled Sunder but hair was that of Nayar, he was stamping through the city, crushing cars, people and anything that came in its way, Karan was next and he ran, jumping over various cricket bats installed on the road, throwing cricket balls from his pocket on the giant whenever he got a chance, the balls never ended, he always had one when he needed it, the bats were of various sizes, some small and some big, on his way he saw a man sitting on the pavement watching TV, not bothered by the giant, he tried calling for help but the man didn't respond, he looked a lot like dad, just a little younger, like from a photo in their drawing room. He keeps running, a taxi approaches him, the driver's face, he can't see but he has his name tattooed on the back of his neck, Yash, it reads. "Drive fast", he yells, the driver floors the pedal but the car doesn't pick up, the giant is catching up, he opens the door of the taxi and jumps outside, but there is no road beneath, he goes into a free fall, it is dark and quiet, disturbed just by his yell, Shivani's phone is ringing, "Can't talk now I am falling", he yells over the phone and throws it, both continue the fall together, "I don't want to die", he keeps on repeating, the bed is wet from his sweat and the half spilled glass of booze, he wakes up with a start, still sweating, still shivering.

Australia's tour of India was still a month away, but there was the Tennis tournament, comparatively easy to bet on, the upsets are few and decent amount of money could be won. Just to pass time and make some cash, he had bet on matches involving the top seeds against the smaller contestants and had won, better than nothing. Yash was back, campaigning against something at the university campus, after work Karan was supposed to meet him at a nearby *Dhaba*, along with some more men, a job had come up and Yash was responsible for gathering the team and completing it. Finally, some action in life for Karan, he was unusually cheery at work and left the office half an hour before time to get some excitement back in his life.

Chapter 14

THE ASSIGNMENT

Sunder Sharma was a land grabber by profession, earlier he worked for other men with money to get plots and lands that they desired in return of handsome rewards but since he had entered politics, thanks to the earned money and contacts, he had hired people under him to do the same. He held considerable land in and around the city but the lust had not waned. He wanted more and now with assembly elections over, it was time to amass more wealth. Sunder was eyeing a disputed land right next to a six lane highway, but he, who owned it, wasn't interested in selling, Sunder couldn't intimidate him because the man had bigger connections with industrialist and people at the center but Sunder was not going to concede. Yash and his team were hired to 'convince' the man, popularly known as VK, to part with his land at a reasonable cost, after all money was not important in matters of mortality; in return they were to get 1 percent of the deal cost, a strong motive to execute the settlement successfully. Sunder's old guns were either holed up in jail or had run away to avoid arrests or getting killed. He had selected this young bunch of men because they were loyal to him and had put up a good show during the elections, also if things went wrong and few needed to be sacrificed, it could be done without worrying too much.

The team of five assembled at the *dhaba* by 9. Being a weekday, it was not crowded and few chronic drunks sat in the corner drinking cheap liquor and eating complimentary peanuts. Yash, Karan and Raja had reached an hour before everybody else to catch up and down a few drinks before the rest arrived. After that 'compromise meeting' under the tree, Raja, short for Rajkiran, had become a regular part of the group, doing odd jobs for Yash and Karan when they were either too busy or didn't think too much of the task.

Five people were a few too many for the task but being in politics, they realized the power in numbers and having more people go together to an assignment gave the guys confidence and a sense of security.

The plan was simple; to barge into VK's office, make the offer, insist on it, and mention the political favors that he will get as a bonus once the deal is done. They knew he was a wealthy man but were sure of their plan, conveniently thought up in 10 minutes while drinking and basing it on the various movies their collective intellect had absorbed. Earlier, Sunder had mildly alluded to the guy's connections but that didn't cause any panic in the young gang consisting of individuals who wanted to attain name and money and they knew that cracking this deal was their ticket to the big league. The plan was executed faster in their head than in reality, the man they were supposed to meet and intimidate was a very busy businessman, he was off to Europe for a month and in his absence there was nobody to talk to and threaten; the guys had no option but to wait which diminished the edge that they had in the beginning of the task. Boredom set in and they stopped following up, by the time they found out that VK was back in the city, it had already been fifteen days since he had arrived and was scheduled to fly off to some place again for a few days. The plan was clearly not working and the guys were getting anxious and annoyed.

It was a chance encounter; Yash, Karan and Raja were hanging around a tea shop, smoking and checking out girls when they spotted an Audi stop a few meters away, while the driver parked the car, the family got down-VK accompanying what looked like his wife and two kids. The guys had seen him in newspaper clippings and at some political gatherings. They didn't want to miss their chance, it had been so long, but the three of them going together at a public place would have raised an alarm, Yash began to volunteer but stopped; "Would any of you want to do it? This can catapult you to popularity in a big way", Before Karan could decide, Raja was on his way to face their target. Yash wasn't sure of Raja's skills but knew well enough that it is better to send someone in to check the waters than jump recklessly; he also knew that in his zeal to please and climb the ladder, Raja will readily agree without thinking.

Nothing happened for the first fifteen minutes since Raja followed them inside a famous restaurant. They were joking if VK gladly asked him to join for dinner and agreed on the deal, Karan tried calling up Raja but he didn't answer, after a few silent minutes, Yash realized something, he ran towards the rear of the building, Karan tried to keep up, not really understanding his friend's intent. The restaurant had a backyard used for keeping trash bins and employee vehicles. By the time they reached, they could see the service door closing, Raja lay there on his face behind one of the trash containers, certainly not dead but severely injured, his lower lip was cut, nose broken and shirt torn. He was breathing but could not speak. They rushed him to the hospital, there was no time to get a first person's account of what had happened but they kind of knew.

Raja had entered the venue not unnoticed. His dressing and the fact that he had turned up alone at a family restaurant was noted by the guard standing outside. Rumors that VK had a stake in the restaurant were not untrue, the staff knew VK well and there was always a private dining arranged for him whenever he visited with family or clients. The restaurant was pretty full but the family section was separated with a frosted glass wall, all the four tables were left vacant and the area was closed for customers. Raja asked one of the waiters about his location but the waiter feigned ignorance. After waiting for about ten minutes to catch sight of the man, he became impatient and began a discussion with the manager which soon turned into a loud debate when manager refused to tell him despite being told who he worked with. The guard manning the door came forward, caught Raja by the arm and asked him to leave quietly; everybody was looking at this guy in a yellow checkered shirt and tight denims. The receptionist made a call and two guys emerged, one of them was VK's driver; while one caught Raja by the back of his neck, the driver, cum bodyguard, wrenched his arm to the back, twisting his forefinger with the thumb, they took him through the kitchen and out the backdoor. "I will fuck your sister." was the last thing that Raja could utter before a head butt blacked him out and a heel to the groin put an end to his perfect day.

CHAPTER 15

FLEETING TIME

It had been two weeks and the boys had not turned up at Sunder's office, they didn't want him to know but realized that nothing was hidden from him and he must have found out about the ill fated diner incident on the same day. They were right; Sunder had waited for them to come up and tell him, he knew what they did was wrong but he also knew that these were the people who will make it right, there was no point in getting angry when being patient could fetch him better rewards. He got a message sent to Yash that he wanted to see his gang before 7. There was no other option but to comply, Raja was reluctant and didn't want to come out in the open yet, but he knew he didn't have a choice, more than the broken face he was afraid of Sunder, who was notorious for ripping people apart in the presence of others and ending their careers for good, there were a lot of road kills who had known the leader at some point in their life.

When the three walked into the office, the conversations died down, there were a couple of government employees sitting there discussing the Medical seat scam when Sunder interjected them and asked them to come back later. Yash closed the door behind them, calm but half expecting Sunder to throw something at them, he had seen it happen before. Karan stood there blankly not really knowing what to expect but he had disappointed people before, he did not want to be Raja right now. "There is a difference between movies and reality, like there is a difference between being brave and being foolish. What you three tried to do was to perform a movie scene in real life which is foolish. I credited you with more sense than that", he pointed at Yash; that was the first and the last time Karan saw fear in Yash's eyes.

The meeting went much better than the three had imagined. There was the chiding and nod of the head with a generous sprinkle of abuses but it was not threatening, more like a mentor's session about how to handle difficult people. They were informed that the restaurant which was chosen by them for the rendezvous was funded by VK as a whitening exercise, he travels with a bodyguard who also happens to be his driver and most of the staff keeps getting transferred within his businesses so they are all loyal to him. They were also advised to not use Sunder's name at all places because if somebody were not intimidated by his name, there was a high probability that that somebody could be harmful. Sunder didn't want to involve himself more than necessary and talked in hints, knowing very well that if stars didn't align well, he could be in the eye of the biggest controversy and in his profession such controversies usually meant the end in more ways than one.

The guys had decided to not act in haste, the initial flop show had made a few things clear; VK was not an average Joe who could be brow beaten into anything against his wish, they were no match for him in a direct battle and if they wanted to please the boss and become big players on the political landscape, they must plan an ambush and force him into submission. Imagine the awe and respect that they would receive from the veterans; they might be recognized all the way to Delhi, who knows! It was time to pull off some kind of a heist.

After the meeting the boys had run out of steam and decided to take a break till they could think up of something. But before the break, there were some things to be taken care of.

Arshad lived on the outskirts of town, his father had worked as a driver and later as a guard at VK's residence; he used to hang out a VK's small trading unit while his father was out running errands for the house before leaving for home late at night with his son. As a child, he enjoyed wearing clothes given out every few months by VK's wife; he also loved the sweets, mostly the leftovers that were given away after the big parties that were frequently hosted at the palatial bungalow. The bigger VK grew the jazzier grew the events. Arshad's fondness for sweets was later replaced by love for imported booze that flowed in gallons at the party. When his father got old, Arshad made sure that he picked up the job as a driver before somebody else got to know of it. He was young and strong which helped him fill in as a bodyguard once VK became too rich to be safe and threat-less. Beating people up had always interested Arshad, he didn't like restraining himself now especially now when he was working for a powerful and influential master. The day when a boy weighing half than him walked in the restaurant and created a ruckus, asking around for boss he was outside, thanks to the guard at the gate else he would have missed the opportunity to rough up the hooligan. It was fun, he had gotten into some serious brawls in the locality where he lived and was no fun anymore but catching the guy, dragging him outside and head butting him with precision gave him a high that no amount of IMFL could give. For all the connections the boy had, nobody turned up to lift his sorry ass from behind the restaurant. He was sure the dog wasn't dead; it would have been in the papers otherwise.

Navratri was around the corner and just like the other who can, Arshad was busy collecting *Chandaa* from the locals to set up a 9 day *Bhandaara* along with his friends. None of the organizes were particularly religious, some didn't even practice Hinduism but organizing such an activity had multiple benefits; the organizers got a lot of fame via free hoardings with their faces on them, they got a free hand from the police and the administration that wanted to look secular and didn't want to obstruct a yearly religious exercise which pretty much let the organizers do whatever they pleased, but the biggest return was the money, the amount they collected and the facilities that they provided in return didn't match well, most of the things were obtained at reduced prices or foe free and this helped them make a good amount of money by the end of the event. As the days got closer, various food camps were being organized across the city, different localities had different faces on flyers and posters, roads were blocked to set up tents from which music blared uninterrupted. Now and then fistfights broke out between rivals or sometimes friends high on dope (they refrained from consuming liquor and non vegetarian food during the nine days, but who would say a no to Lord Shiva's gift).

Raja had not forgotten the guy who had left a bad scar on his face, he still got headaches and watery eyes from the assault, sometimes they were the tears of humiliation but mostly the headaches troubled him. After getting to know the background story of VK, he and friends did a lot of checks and searches to know the whereabouts of Arshad, some of them loitered outside the factory and offices as innocent smokers to identify him and then trail him. The trail had yielded results and a guy had followed Arshad till his *mohalla*; going closer was dangerous and would have raised an alarm. Now it was time to wait.

CHAPTER 16

BAPTIZED BY BLOOD

Karan had come home to visit his parents, it had been a while since he had seen them and with festivals around the corner, he thought he will visit and get away from the hectic office schedule. Nothing much was happening in his personal life, betting had been on as usual and the money used to come in more often than not. His affiliations and contacts had made quite a few places free for him which further saved cash. He was a changed guy now, his thin frame had a slight belly and he used to leave home for cigarette breaks. Hanging out with politicians had made him somewhat of a talker. He talked to his mom and dad more than he used to and entertained their queries about getting married and settling down. It was announced that they had begun searching for a girl of their caste who could look after him and their home. He would just add timed, non-committal nods and let the topic wear out by itself. He wasn't sure how long would he be able to carry out such behavior calmly; it was a Friday when he got a call, he just listened for a while, said ok and hung up. He had already been home for four days, longer than usual, so when he decided to leave the next day citing work, the parents didn't complain. He dropped the calm and cheery face as soon as the bus departed carrying him to the city.

The nine days were over and the people were drunk; it was time to burn Ravan's effigy on the night of Dusshera and also celebrate the money made out of the nine days of religious obeisance of the faithful. The Ravan was about a hundred feet high, his eyes gleaming with LED lights made in China while his body contained gunpowder that would put a suicide bomber to shame. The evil lord was to be assassinated by Sunder Sharma, the noted leader who had arrived dressed in sparkling white *Kurta-Pajama*, escorted by his own troop of bodyguards and followers. Arshad was behind the building busy downing a few with a couple of his friends, organizing any event required money, and this money was taken by people either subtly or with force, whatever made them part with it. Nothing below 500 was accepted but there was no ceiling. Under the influence of alcohol and security of his own locality, Arshad didn't notice the crowd, it was time to shoot the Ravan in his naval and symbolize the victory of good over evil. His friends had begun walking towards the structure along with the announcement of the arrival of *Sri* Ram while Arshad hung around waiting for one of his girlfriends to steal herself from the crowd and come over to him. The arrow had been shot and he could hear the fireworks, the head of Ravan exploded and it was about then that Arshad felt a stabbing pain in the back, he could feel his shirt getting wet and warm while the exit wound at the front hurt like a bitch. He knew he had been shot, the liquor wore off but neither the painful yell nor the sound of the bullet was heard. With the next burst came a bullet from close range, into the head. Arshad never saw his murderer.

It was widely covered in the evening papers and local news channels. The murder of a driver who some papers called a local goon made headlines for days to come, there were no leads but according to the police the victim's name was Arshad and a local gang war did him in. Arrangements were made to make sure that none of the papers mentioned him being the driver of VK who reportedly was out of the country and unreachable for comment. Sunder, the chief guest called the incident unfortunate and condemned the criminal act on such a pious day, he also didn't forget to mention how there were members of the other political party who were jealous and intended to disrupt peace and harmony that his party had inspired amongst people of the city. The news stayed hot for a while but with no real leads or witness it was taken over by other stories.

On the night of *Dushhera*, Sunder's entourage to the venue made sure that he came out all guns blazing with his power on display in its full glory. His Innova was followed by an open jeep carrying his supporters dressed in party colors and yelling out his name. In that crowd of overzealous supporters were Karan, Yash and Raja. Raja had grown a scraggly beard and shaved his head and with a hoodie he looked unrecognizable. As soon as the gang reached the venue, Karan jumped out and disappeared while Raja moved out to the parking and accompanied the driver who waited in the vehicle. Yash went out with Sunder and the rest, keeping an eye out for Arshad. Karan just strolled around without being noticed, he was still comparatively unknown unlike Yash who was seen as Sunder's go to man for things that involved people and force. He walked around the place knowing well that one of the key hosts of this entire setup can't be away. After strolling through the entire perimeter he walked to the back of a two storey sports complex to pee, that's where he heard few men laughing and sharing jokes, they were mostly making fun of the chief guest and sharing stories of the action from the past ten days. 'Arshad bhai', somebody called out in the dark, his eyes, now adjusted to the dark could see the silhouettes of six people, presumably drinking. "Let's go up front, some good chicks I hear", the voice completed. You guys carry on I need to take care of some things, all but one got up and began laughing. What luck! Karan thought, he messaged Raja to come over, the guys had checked out the place a night before so that everybody knew where to be if called. Within the next two minutes Raja was there, almost invisible, Karan stood behind a bush that was big enough to keep them out of sight. The guys were out of sight and Karan's job was done, he moved to the jeep in case things went wrong. Raja waited behind the bush, every minute seemed unending. He had never done something like this before; brawls and fistfights are fine but killing someone was going to be a new addition to his resume. "The bastard deserves it for breaking my nose, the motherfucker", he yelled inside his head. Arshad sat there texting the girl unaware of his immediate demise while Raja cursed Sunder for taking too long to play out the final war scene. And then it began, as soon as he heard the announcement, his senses became sharper, he had not drank for two days to be as sober as possible and only smoked a joint to calm his nerves and be alert. With the first sound of small crackers he moved rapidly forward, tiptoeing in his canvas shoes while Arshad was immersed in the phone screen, his usually acute senses dulled by fatigue, drinks and overconfidence. A second before the head of the effigy burst with a loud noise followed by roar of the onlookers, his sixth sense asked him to turn back but before he could, he felt a searing stab in his back and his face, if somebody could have seen, had not an expression of pain but of shock; the shock of dying so suddenly, about the futility of it all, he was also angry and knew that only if his friends could see him, he would survive, the thought was never completed and the bullet ended a promising criminal's life. By the time his girlfriend arrived, Raja had vanished; she couldn't spot him in the dark and dialed his number which rang on the ground. She yelled, tried to wake him up but it was late. By the time Arshad's friends arrived, the girl had left, leaving the carcass unclaimed and alone.

The guys ran away for a long vacation, they knew nothing would happen but didn't want to risk anything. They had decided to not tell Sunder their plans, knowing well that they had his support as long as he was not made aware of things. Involvement in petty issues like murder were not befitting of a politician.

Chapter 17

Kidnapping and Other Such Crimes

Two months had gone by since the Dusshera murder, mystery was never solved, but to put the press and people at peace, the police had arrested some other criminals and declared the case as closed. This had two benefits, the three men who were arrested were local thugs who had been at large looting and killing for money and catching them from the same locality, for a crime that they had not committed, gave a small victory to the law and proved the capability of the cops to close a case successfully. Nobody cared if those men were guilty of Arshad's murder but knowing their track record and the rarity of successful solution of criminal cases everybody was happy that at least some people were caught.

Raja was back to town, not because he enjoyed being there but because there was nowhere else to go. He looked different, he had lost weight, had long hair that reached his shoulders and his face was partially hidden with a mane that was strategically nurtured to hide him in plain sight. It was not just his appearance that had changed, he was not the same guy who had sweated with a gun in his hand, he was not the guy who wanted to please people, he was a darker version of the boy everybody knew. He rarely met people, only Yash sometimes. He had moved to a different field of work, and his meetings with Sunder were solitary and discreet; nobody discussed his work anymore. Karan would occasionally see him at Yash's house, they would exchange few sentences and he would be gone. He lived alone now, even his family wasn't aware of his whereabouts. Cut off from everybody and everything, booze and drugs kept him conveniently numb to everything around him. He had bought a four wheeler, a black Scorpio with tinted windows and he lived with a woman nobody else had seen or met. "What's wrong with Raja?" Karan asked Yash one day, he was pretty sure that he had lost his mind because of all the alcohol that he consumed and maybe he couldn't take the guilt of killing a person, he had seen such things happen on television. He was right. That night after the murder, Raja had tried reaching Sunder who had not received his call. He couldn't sleep that night and hid on the terrace of a sparsely populated building, sure that the police will catch him and send him to jail to rot for life. He sat till early morning trying to think of what he could do but couldn't think straight, at times he thought of jumping off the terrace, you don't arrest a dead person. He was angry with himself, he never got to celebrate killing that bastard and now when he should be drinking and dancing he sat here feeling guilty. At 4:00 am he received a text from Yash to meet him at a garden in next ten minutes, he knew that place well, Sunder did his morning walks there, he had no money but he knew how to unlock old two wheelers; it was still dark and even the weak watchman was asleep, he spotted an old CD100, unlocked it and rode it away as fast as he could, not worrying if he was seen; it is better to be caught for theft than for murder. When he reached the garden, there were already a few people stretching and performing *asanas*. He circled the garden till he spotted a familiar bike, it was Yash's. They met without a smile; "You look like shit, don't be scared, Sunder bhai knows about what you did, for everybody's security it is better that you leave the town within an hour, don't come back for some days". "But"! Raja began nervously, afraid that he had been asked to leave and now with no friends or money he would definitely be caught. Yash slipped an envelope in Raja's sweaty hands. "Leave now", he said and rode away. The envelope had 50,000 rupees, enough to take him wherever he wanted, but he couldn't think straight, he was relieved and overcome with emotions. He rode to the bus stand, and took a bus to a village where his cousin lived. He couldn't think of any place else, didn't know anybody else, he wasn't even sure if the cousin still lived there or was alive but he left anyway. After bidding time, watching more news and reading more papers than he had done in his life, he was sure that the police had failed to crack the case; he wanted to get back to the city but waited to hear back from the guys, he hoped they would call. They did; it was the 50th day of his exile when he got a message, "8:00 pm, terrace, Saturday". He was happy, he had been called but he couldn't muster a smile. Raja preferred traveling in the night and he took a late night bus to the city on Friday. By the time the bus arrived, it was only 3pm and scared of stepping outside and reaching before time, Raja lay down in the waiting room, trying to catch on some sleep. There were other people lying around on makeshift mattresses and bed sheets. He occupied a bench, put his shoes under his head and fell asleep. Tuned out from the noise of the buses and commuters, he got up at 7 and realized how much he enjoyed the noise of the city; the silence of village had given him creeps, thanks to the bottle he could sleep at all.

On the terrace he was welcomed by Yash, Karan and couple more guys who he didn't really know but he had seen them earlier. It was cold and Rum was the drink of the night, everybody wore layered clothing but not Raja, he hadn't taken any clothes in a hurry and there were no real malls in the village to buy outfits of choice. He carried a blanket though, not just to fight the cold but also to stay out of sight; his paranoia had grown, he wanted to hug his friends, share jokes just like the old days but couldn't, all of what he wanted to do only translated as a faint smile on his face. Sensing discomfort, Yash nodded to the guys and they left, leaving just Karan and him with their old friend. They could sense heaviness in chilly air, their jokes didn't work and soon there was nothing left to talk about. Raja had gulped down almost a quarter of bottle which was beginning to take effect, he loosened up a little and began speaking, narrating his village experience, how he would always be grateful to Sunder and Yash for lending him the money, he still had most of it, blowing the rest on booze and food; he talked about not regretting doing what he did and he was braver now, then he began to cry. Boys don't cry, especially the ones who are in their line of work, Yash and Karan didn't know what to do so they just let him weep hoping it would be cathartic, the three of them sat and drank in silence for about thirty minutes. Raja's mind was full of questions, but despite all the booze he couldn't ask Yash directly, maybe Yash didn't know either and was just the relay man. It was half an hour past midnight when Yash suddenly got up,

"Let's go", he announced, gulped the remaining drink in the glass and started descending the stairs, Raja got up laboriously and followed his friend, he looked at Karan who just nodded. When they reached downstairs, Yash was waiting near Karan's bike with his keys. Karan rode, and Raja sat between him and Yash, asking more questions was futile. They rode in the dark, doing between 60 and 80 for fifteen minutes or so, could have been more but nobody was keeping track of time, soon they took a path off the city, the roads became narrower and the darkness was only pierced by passing heavy vehicles. They soon slowed down in front of a farm house; it was dark, and they slid in through a smaller gate that was partially open.

Sunder sat near his pool, finishing what looked like the last glass for the day, there had been more people from the looks of the tables around him. The guys stood behind him waiting for him to finish his glass, he did, turned around and looked at them. "I was about to retire for the night, you came on time", he looked at Raja with a face that looked softer and empathic; "Good to see you back, come with me, while the two of you can sit here, drink some good scotch and take a walk in the lawns, we won't be long". Before they could understand, Sunder put an arm on Raja's shoulder and took him inside the house. Yash and Karan was surprised but didn't really care, they were used to the strange ways of

Sunder, besides there was a lot of Chivas left in the bottle; they soon picked up clean glasses and began from where they had left on the terrace. It was close to 2:30 when Raja got down, either it was the good liquor or their friend really looked much better. He smiled, took a swig directly from the bottle, "let's go home".

India was scheduled to play England in a three T20 series followed by three ODI's and two tests. The games were supposed to begin in the evening, with all the guys in the circle interested in betting most other extracurricular activities were put on hold. This series was important for Karan, he had finally resigned from his job and gotten into real estate as a deal broker, there had been no matches off late and his lifestyle could not be sustained for long by a job that didn't give any fixed income; he had gotten into it knowing that any deal could get him a lot of money as commission, a lot of his friends were doing it and just one successful deal in a month was enough to see them through thirty days of joblessness till they could crack another one. He already had contacts with guys who had properties in the city; all he needed were buyers which he would find soon. Yash had decided to watch the game with friends, he wasn't really into betting, and did it for fun and make some money now and then. Karan decided to stay home and watch the opening match alone; all the profits in previous matches had given him enough confidence to take his own decisions. To take the edge off his nervousness, he had devised a way, he would roll a joint at the time of the toss and chug a glass of whisky with soda, thus giving things enough time to kick in by the time the match began. He believed that this secret formula of his kept him sane and helped him take objective decisions, quite contrary to the findings that alcohol's effect on cerebral cortex impairs judgment. T20 is a risky format to bet and the professional bookies advise to just watch the game for the fun of it but this was a series of desperation for Karan. It had been over a month since he resigned after throwing a cup of coffee on Nayar's shirt after being pulled up in public for being the most non-performing employee in the company. In a fit of rage and knowing well that the consequences won't be too drastic, Karan threw the beverage on his superior and for the effect walked off the office, the salary for the month had already been credited last week and he knew that the management won't worry about getting back at him.

With only fifteen thousand remaining in his bank account he began watching the game with conviction, he still had a credit of two lacs with Inzamam which he would soon cash out by the end of the Indian tour; he was sure people betted on T20 games and made a lot of tax free money, this was his time. Some wanted power for which they could kill and plunder, some wanted girls and fame but he wanted money, a lot of it and he didn't have time to wait for it till he was old, it had to be done now.

His first session was at 10 over mark, with India batting and Dhawan and Sharma in form, India was 75 by the end of the 7th over, he was sure they would cross 110 by the end of the tenth, the English bowling looked pretty toothless against the in-form India. However a couple of tight overs and two wickets in the ninth over-a run out and a caught behind off an unplayable delivery from Anderson left India with only a 105 off the ten overs. The match was not lost for India but Karan was down by 15,000. "No big deal"! He, powered by hash and malt, thought to himself, there was still a lot of match left. By the end of that game, Karan had recovered some money and with a fifty percent record, was only down by 10,000. This amount used to worry the old Karan, but the new one was sure that he will cover it; the credit with the bookie relieved him of the fear that he might be chased and asked for money. Had Karan taken this as an omen and refrained from betting on the next two games, he would have been a happier man. But with one third of the tour over and only ODI series to go (he wasn't comfortable with betting in tests); Karan was down by 45,000 rupees. He was nervous but there was no need to click the panic button yet.

———◆•◆•◆———

"Something needs to be done", said Yash, while smoking a cigarette, Sunder hasn't forgotten about the assignment he gave to us. Since that first meeting the guys had stayed away from VK, Arshad's murder was more a vendetta than a way to reach the businessman. Karan, Raja and three others were part of the discussion, after some impractical ideas and silence, Raja spoke for the first time; "We need to kidnap somebody - his kid". The chill and the calm in his voice made it clear that he was not joking, everybody knew by now that he had become a professional shooter and worked for Sunder and his allies on jobs that required anonymity, unlike earlier, he was speaking out of experience and everybody heard intently.

———◆•◆•◆———

CHAPTER 18

THE MOVE

VK had two daughters, the older one, Kirti, was in 10th while the younger one, Keira, was in 5th standard. Theoretically it was the younger one who could be kidnapped but doing that was as difficult as meeting VK had been. She was driven to and from school by the driver, the house was heavily guarded and nothing was visible through the high walls, the servants lived inside and had their quarters there so them being manipulated was highly improbably. But there had to be a way, someone for sure could be bought, the only thing that needed to be figured out was, who?

After Arshad's death, VK had sent a sum of money to his parents to make sure that they didn't have to suffer in their old age. He had hired a driver by the name of Jagan; Jagan was from a small village in Andhra Pradesh, his mother had died while giving him birth and his dad, a farmer, had committed suicide due to destroyed crop and mounting interest. Jagan had been a cab driver in Hyderabad and had been VK's chaperone for fifteen days on one of his business trips. After Arshad's murder, VK wanted to employ somebody who didn't have any ties in the city hoping that this will keep him away from local gang wars; he had been unaware of the real reason behind Arshad's death and didn't really have too much time to delve into such petty matters. On his part, Jagan himself had problems of his own; since his father passed away he only went to the village once, for the funeral and left the village even before the pyre cooled down. He used to drink but despair pushed him into ways he thought could alleviate pain and anguish, but such ways, ironically, could not be afforded by those with no extra money at their disposal. To make more money, he gambled and had debts, but the stars were just right when he got a call from one of the guys he had driven for a fortnight or so; he remembered the guy, had given him a thousand rupees over and above the fare set by his travel company. So when he got a call, 10,000 a month, free stay and food, he hopped into the train and did not show up for work the next day.

Jagan's job was not too complex but involved long hours; there were two drivers in the house, one who drove Mrs. VK to various kitties and parties, at least three a week and Jagan who drove VK and shared kid's duties with Mrs. VK's driver. His duty began at 6 in the morning, to drop VK to a garden nearby for a morning walk, his bodyguards followed on a bike. He dropped VK back at 8 then took the girls to school at 8:30, VK's office was far off so they left at 9:30 and reached work at 11. The entire day went off on the road doing various assignments of office and home and the day ended around 10 or 11 in the night; he had a television in his quarter, a comfortable one room plus kitchen and bath where he watched a movie with a nightcap before retiring, to begin the cycle all over again. He got a day off every two weeks to do whatever he pleased; he usually slept on that day.

One such day, Jagan went to have a haircut, he kept it like one of his favorite movie stars, long sidelocks, naturally curly hair longer at the back and falling on the eyes in the front, all of this paired with a neat pencil moustache over his lip. There were expensive stores around but he went to the one that costed him 20 rupees, 10 more for a shave. On his way back, he decided to pick up a quarter for the day. It was unusually crowded at the liquor store, Jagan got in line and tried to get in; the men standing next to him objected and asked him to back off and wait for his turn. Jagan ignored and continued to pass on the 50 rupee note to the store keeper; suddenly, before he could realize, one of the guys punched him on the face. Soon everybody joined in to watch, after all what's more exciting than people fighting. Jagan tried to fight back but lost his balance and fell down the flight of stairs; the guy who had punched him mounted him and took a knife out when suddenly one of the guys from the crowd caught his hand and the other took the knife off him. Understanding that the brawl had lost steam, people went off to whatever they were doing. Jagan got up in shock and thanked Yash and Karan for saving him from a certain death. They picked him up and sponsored a beer to calm his nerves. Jagan was very thankful and exchanged numbers with Karan, promising that they will meet over drinks someday.

Next week he met up with Yash and Karan at the same wine shop and they shared a few beers in the parking. Jagan told them his story and how he had ended up in the city. They enlightened the driver about the cruelties of his employer and how the news in the market was that he had gotten his ex driver bumped off for stealing money. They also told him how his working hours were harder than those of local drivers and he should definitely ask for a raise. This went on for a few weeks and by now the three were good friends; Jagan partially believed what his life saving friends told him about this master and had begun feeling annoyed with all the riches that he could see but never have; all the money being wasted on shopping and parties and clothes for kids while the rest of the staff lived like slaves. He barely talked to the rest of the staff at home, he never had time.

India's tour of England had been as disastrous for Karan as it had been for team India. He had lost a sum of 85,000 and really had no way of paying it back, at one point he contemplated running away, but where to? He felt safe in the city and with so many connections, he was sure there will be a way out even if in form of some loan. As the plan of abducting progressed, everybody involved knew that there would be a lot of money to be made on the side, besides getting signatures on documents that Sunder wanted; Karan was sure that this one hit will be the answer to his financial woes.

"Are you married"? Yash asked Jagan one night while sitting with his back to a moldy wall to the rear of the liquor store. "I would have but didn't have enough money to go on with it, I do want to marry though", Jagan replied candidly. "How important is money for you?" Questioned Karan, guiding the discussion that had been practiced several times over the rooftop; "Money is God", Jagan answered, with a tinge of bitterness in his voice, while a flashback of his poor village, and his father's funeral went through his head. His guard was down, he trusted these two guys who had saved him, he put a hand around Yash's shoulder while gulping down a tenth of a beer bottle in one go. "I want to be rich, not work as a driver for these bastards; I want to drive my own car and take my own kids to school, can you make me rich?" He asked them, half begging. "There is a plan, but we don't think you will be able to pull it off", Karan added with a hint of disappointment in his voice; "Yes, you are too loyal and too soft", added Yash. Jagan looked incensed but he didn't say anything for a while, both the boys exchanged quiet glances while the driver looked nervously at his watch. "I should leave, need to get up early tomorrow", with that he got up and started walking. Behind his back, he could hear the two arguing, Yash thought that Jagan was too kind to be a rich man while Karan said that he had the passion and he will agree to become big someday.

The road was crowded on account of a political rally, Jagan was chauffeuring VK to his office in his Merc on a busy road when suddenly a biker with a family of four cut into his lane, with his mind wandering, Jagan spotted the bike at the last moment, and overcompensated by swerving to the right and in the process scraping the front of the car; because he couldn't stop at the turn he stopped a few meters ahead, pulling the car to the corner. VK sat in the car unpleased while Jagan got down. It was a nasty scratch, the paint had come off and there was a dent as well. VK asked him to lower down the window while Jagan stood outside, he could see the anger on his boss's face. "Is it bad?"

Jagan partially nodded in affirmation, VK got out, looked at the damage for a little while, suddenly he just turned and slapped the driver square on the jaw, Jagan staggered a little, he was shocked as he hadn't seen that coming. "Drop me, take the car to the showroom's workshop, get a quotation for the repair and bring it to me; you better pray that it's not too much because all of it would be deducted from your salary." Jagan stood there while VK got back to his seat. "Now don't stand there like a fool, that's not going to repair it." He walked back to the driver's seat, head hanging low, his eyes fixed at nothing in particular on the ground and feet heavy. He knew it was his mistake but a slap on the road and salary deduction was overkill and he was angry, all the guilt of scratching the car was overpowered by a feeling of anger and revenge. He didn't even realize when the entire day went by; he kept on planning ways of killing his boss without getting caught. Should he slam the car right on into a wall, it would look like an accident, but what if God is watching and he dies and that bastard VK survives. No, it must be fool proof, should he take off from a bridge drowning him, while he swims off, it can be an accident. Blow the whole fucking house up using a leaking gas cylinder. He fantasized about ways all day till he went to sleep; it helped alleviate the bruised ego.

Jagan waited the entire week for VK to apologize but nothing came, this enraged him even more. Let's meet up tonight; Karan got a message which he showed to Yash who just smiled. That night, Jagan reached the store earlier than usual, he knew the guys will come at their usual hour but he was too anxious to stay back, time passed, he called once but both the numbers were switched off, he waited patiently, no call back, the phones were still not on, he waited till he could wait no more and left leaving his beer unfinished. "Have we gone too far? What if he doesn't show up again?" Karan asked Yash sitting in an SUV with tinted windows watching Jagan leave. He wanted to jump out and stop Jagan and tell him that they were just testing him, he wanted to get him on the team and carry out extortion soon, he wanted the money, he wanted a good night's sleep. But Yash had clasped his wrist, not too tightly, but tightly enough to affirm his position. "We won't meet him when he wants us to; he has to come back when we call him."

They got calls the next morning as well, but didn't answer. Jagan had gotten desperate, he had thought taking revenge upon VK would have been easy with the other two guys but they were not receiving his calls, why? Was it something he had said the other night? Did he make them angry? Should he go back to the store and find them? What if they aren't there? What if they are? Won't he look needy? He was so caught up in thoughts that he didn't hear the phone vibrating. Friday night, 9 pm, same place, read the message from Karan. He looked at the calendar today, it was Wednesday, and there was still one day. Why didn't you guys show up that night? He messaged, but there was no reply. What the fuck! He thought, I won't go there; but he did. He didn't want to go first and tell them that what they did was wrong, but he couldn't keep himself from it, so he decided to go late but still reached with 5 minutes to 9. The guys were not there, he thought of leaving but as soon as he turned around, there stood Yash grinning, holding a beer bottle in his hand. "Let's sit", Yash said calmly, like an instruction. Jagan involuntarily followed him, behind him was Karan, carrying two bottles. He kept the bottles down and began before sitting completely; "So, what was so urgent the other night?" He asked, trying to sound as unapologetic as Yash. "Yeah well you guys certainly didn't care", nobody said anything. "We have to leave for something important in half an hour", Yash said offhandedly. Jagan couldn't carry out this charade anymore; he spoke about the insult and his murdering fantasy. Both the guys were surprised at this lucky break. They were only psyching Jagan out so that he agrees to their plan but they were sure now he would yield quicker. "You still want to be rich?" Asked Yash in his usual flat tone; "What?", "Do you still want to be rich and avenge your insult?" "Yes, I do", then we can help you.

They held the next meeting the very next night. Just the four of them; They introduced Raja to Jagan as an important man who could intimidate anybody and the play had to be set in motion.

CHAPTER 19

KIDNAPPING KEIRA

VK was supposed to fly to Mumbai for a day, usually he was pretty secretive about his travel plans, a lot of his employees never knew when he was in and when he wasn't, this kept them on the heels at all hours. He shared his itinerary with a very few people, one of them had to be his driver. The flight was at 6 in the morning and VK was dropped to the terminal an hour earlier. Everybody was asleep at the house; they were so used to VK's travel that nobody bothered with the perfunctory farewells or welcomes. It was the weekend, and the kids had planned evening shopping with mom and a dine-out in the night once they got back from school; a couple of Mrs. VK's friends also joined in. Jagan's duty was to take the ladies around and wait in the parking lot till they got back, he hated the waiting part, and there was a lot of waiting to be done.

Jagan was bringing Kirti and Keira back from school so that they could get ready for the girl's night out, while their mother was attending a kitty at hotel nearby. "Drop me to Pooja's house", Kirti instructed Karan as soon as she got in the car. "But baby madam had..", Jagan tried to complete his sentence in broken and heavily accented English. "Don't argue I'll be back soon, just do it", Kirti interjected.

Pooja didn't live far from the school, but Jagan had been instructed to first drop Keira, the younger one, at the hotel with mommy so that she had an excuse for leaving the party early and then go home with Kirti. Jagan dropped Kirti at her friend's place and took the less busy ring road to the hotel. It was just past noon and there were not a lot of vehicles on the road, people were either at work or at home, best time to take such an expensive car to a higher gear that it deserved. The hotel was not too far, it would take Jagan 20 minutes to drop Keira who was sitting right next to him watching the strays and the people go by, lost in her own world, tired and sleepy from the harsh day at school; there was a truck right ahead of the Audi, ambling in the right lane, Jagan honked but the aged truck rolled along without the will to accelerate or the ability to swiftly move aside, Jagan cursed and tried overtaking the truck from the right, a routine maneuver but just as he was about to surpass the vehicle and get ahead, the truck accelerated, hitting the car from the driver's side and it didn't stop immediately, the mammoth took the dainty car with it to a distance after which the car just skidded on into a pole, precariously tilted to one side; there were shards of glass everywhere, the expensive car was destroyed and irreparable, the axles had become perpendicular to the car, the front had become unhinged and there was smoke coming out of the engine, but no fire. On a slow afternoon, the incident took some time to collect an audience, by then the truck driver had fled, as is usually the case and Jagan, who had fainted, was revived. There was nobody else in the car and he was rushed to a hospital. By the time the cops arrived, Jagan was already gone, the phantom truck stood there without a license plate or any sign of people in it. There were no closed circuit cameras that could be checked for footage. Soon it was found out that the car belonged to VK and the man who was severely injured was his driver; the case could not be taken casually and brushed under the carpet anymore.

When Jagan got up, he was still under the effect of sedatives and couldn't think straight, last thing that he remembered was a loud horn and him trying to swerve the wheel. He closed his eyes again which were opened by the noise around him, his head was throbbing with pain, his right hand hung through a bandage but he couldn't feel anything; there was a bruise on his temple and cheek burned from abrasion of some kind, a familiar sensation that he had experienced several times as a child while falling off his friend's bicycle. But that was it, the car was robust and the airbag had saved his skull from crashing into the steering wheel.

"Jagan, get up, open your eyes", the voice sounded familiar, it was his boss's voice. "He'll surely yell at him about the damaged car", he thought; he didn't realize but it was his second day at the hospital, the first 15 hours were spent in a deep slumber but the ones after were mildly painful and nauseating. He opened his eyes slowly, in front of him stood VK who had taken a flight back home as soon as he got the news on the evening of the accident, boss's wife and an inspector of some high rank. He tried to get up but couldn't. "Where is Keira?"

———◆•◉•◆———

The warehouse was far out in the city; it lay abandoned and was occupied by rodents and pigeons that had the entire place to themselves. At night people sat behind the walls and drank to their heart's content, hiding from the law, the society and reality. The 15 foot gate remained locked from outside and a guard sat there to discourage squatters, thieves and sex offenders from using the place. There were no windows and no ventilation. The unmaintained roof was highest on top and slanted to both sides, starting from 80 feet at the apex and 15 feet at the ends. The guards kept on changing, the job was not very lucrative to begin with and nothing could beat the boredom. The last guard had gone back home asking for a leave and the owner of the warehouse had appointed two new guards, but they were different; bigger, well fed and mean looking the guys had moved to the warehouse a week before the girl was to be brought in. The place was cleaned up from the inside, just enough to make it inhabitable. The girl arrived right after dusk. It was dark and the shepherds nearby had gone back with their cattle. In the absence of electricity the area was quickly sinking into darkness. Safari arrived with four people; Yash and Karan were two of those. The girl lay in the back, tied at the ankles and the wrists, a cloth crudely stuffed in her mouth; this was a mere precaution as she had not woken up after the accident. This was good as they didn't have to worry too much about being suspected but bad because they didn't know if she was seriously hurt. But there was no time to check.

After dropping Kirti, Jagan had texted Karan about his whereabouts asking if they should go ahead with the plan. The boys had not replied as they didn't want to leave any message trails. Unknown even to Jagan, a bike had tailed his Audi, easily identified by the VIP number, the truck parked under a tree was set in motion by a mercenary who was doing this only for the money, unconcerned about the bigger picture. He had already been paid and was told to run away once his job was done. The driver of the truck had confirmed the car in the rear view and slowed down to let the car catch up, he had anticipated the car's move out of experience and as soon as the car overtook him he made his move. The brief was very clear, he didn't know who was in the car but whoever he or she was must not be run over, only injured. As soon as the truck struck the car, the driver ran away and disappeared in the bushes nearby; the roads were pretty deserted for anybody to chase him. Right at the time of impact the bikes were leveled with the car, one had Karan and the other had Yash on it riding with two more on each bike just to be sure. The car had swerved away a little too much and they had to accelerate while making sure that they don't get caught under it. As soon as the car stopped, the guys got off the bike like concerned citizens and surrounded the vehicle. The glass on the driver's side was shattered and Jagan's hand hung out limply, three guys stood on the side of Keira while the other two on the side of the driver, with people still deciding what to do, Yash pulled out the driver who was safely taken out of the car, he quickly unbuckled the girl's seatbelt and passed her out of the other door. Karan picked her up, she was light, and quickly sat behind one of the guys on the bike and they left. People had started to stop now but nobody understood what's going on. Jagan the driver was laid down on the sidewalk as a distraction and everybody surrounded him. Karan's bike had taken a detour to a workshop close by where the Safari waited for them. The plan was to let the girl be in the vehicle till the sun sets before they drive her to the warehouse. Meanwhile Jagan was rushed to the hospital and by the time the police arrived Yash and the others had disappeared. VK's absence from the town had given them an advantage; the cops had not gotten on the tail immediately.

Jagan recollected the incident when VK asked him about Keira. "What do you mean where is she?" She must have been injured but the robust car and seatbelt made sure that she should've been in the car even after the accident. The police couldn't ask him a lot of questions, he couldn't add anything new to what they had witnessed and they were sure he was not lying; he was too dazed and confused for that. Everybody had left, leaving him in the hospital, he wasn't sure who would be paying the bills, he was afraid that they won't discharge him if he didn't pay. His phone was destroyed in the accident; the police had not found it. There was no way to get in touch with Yash and Karan; he didn't remember their numbers to use the hospital phone. While driving he had waited for their call; suddenly it hit him, what if it was them in the truck? The girl was missing, she was not injured, nobody remembered seeing her, he was taken out of the car by few men who couldn't be traced, a lot of this, if pondered over, sounded really suspicious; did the guys do it? Did they want to kidnap the girl without even caring if he died or lived? He needed to find answers to all of it, the injuries were not severe and he would be discharged in a day's time if everything stays stable, he was told. The day he was about to be discharged, the reserve driver came to pick him up. VK was at the IG's office, he informed Jagan and told him that he didn't have to worry about hospital's expenses, they were all paid for. Jagan never found out how much was the bill but looking at the hospital and the services that he got, the room that was better than his house, he was sure it was a lot of money. Once home, he guiltily slipped to his quarters without being noticed. The atmosphere of the house seemed heavy and he didn't see the other car, he felt exhausted and just wanted to sleep; life had been bad as it is but this seemed like a nightmare. Though tired and in pain, he couldn't sleep, he took his medicine and floated to an uneasy slumber. Turning on his cot, he could see the face of little Keira. He didn't talk to her much but she always kept on chattering with her sister or parents, her smile that irritated him earlier, haunted him now. His body needed rest but his mind asked for answers, he slept all night.

Next morning he got dressed for work but by then VK had left; the guards informed him that everybody was looking for Keira; it was in the papers, the accident and the case of missing daughter. VK didn't want the news of missing to go public but he had no other option. Manhunt was on for no one in particular, all the usual kidnappers were rounded up but nobody could tell much, all the low lying areas, all the places where lawlessness flourished were raided but nothing. Sunder released a statement condemning the act and praising the police for doing everything to rescue the daughter of the city.

————◆•◆•◆————

Chapter 20

Holed Out

It had been two days since the kidnapping; the girl was in the warehouse, distraught and scared. She knew she had been kidnapped; they fed her from time to time and gave her water to make sure that she didn't die. They couldn't afford to kill her else they will lose the plot so she was treated better than the other victims. Yash and Karan had gone back to the city so that they could keep an eye on the news and know about developments. Two guys were instructed to stay back and make sure that the girl stays; she was too young to hold any sexual interest for the guys and they made sure that nobody gets close to the place. Food for the night and the next day was brought every evening when some guy from the city would ride in with news and food. Keira was sad, she didn't eat initially but then understood that starving wasn't a solution, she couldn't have escaped like they showed in the movies. There were no windows or weak walls, the kidnappers never went anywhere for her to try and escape. There was a makeshift toilet at the back of the warehouse for its employees and she had to use it, she hated that the most. On the second day, more people walked in and the call was made.

The plan was simple, to call up VK, inform him that they had his daughter and ask him for money, the sum was intended to be so high that even he would negotiate, once the negotiations began, Sunder will step in and offer his help to VK, in return he would ask for the land he had always wanted, he was certain that VK wouldn't mind giving the land away as long as he got his daughter back. Asking for the land in return of the girl had obvious complications and the trail would lead directly to Sunder.

The first call was made at midnight, nobody had slept in the house for two days, there were no trails, no witnesses, no footage and no motive. The police were looking but just because there was pressure from top, they didn't really care, several kidnappings tale place all year for all kind of motives and very few are solved. Had this not been a rich man's daughter, the superiors wouldn't have shown any interest. Late at night VK sat alone in his room, drinking. His wife was with Kirti who had been crying herself to sleep since she had heard the news and blaming herself for getting down at Pooja's house. It was Friday; the call was made from an untraceable number on VK's mobile phone. Had it been a known number he wouldn't have answered, but looking at the screen he did.

"Hello"

"You must have been expecting this call; sorry we were a little caught up feeding you daughter, she is too fussy. Anyway, start arranging for a hundred crores by, will call you again".

"Hello, but.."

VK spoke to nobody at the other end. He knew the smaller cops won't be able to do much and he didn't have such kind of cash ready. He had to call up the ones higher up to reach the kidnappers, to contact them and negotiate Keira's release. He called up the Commissioner of Police and informed him about the call that he got. It was late in the night but the officer knew better than ignoring the call of a guy from whom his department got a lot of private aid. He had been out at a party and there the case of kidnapping was discussed, Sunder had been there and he had offered his help in trying to negotiate with the people once they called. The commissioner let VK know about the offer to help; of all the people! VK thought but didn't say much. This could work, there was no point in getting people from Delhi involved, they wouldn't be much help and it might just piss of the kidnappers or put them in panic which may harm his daughter. As soon as he hung up, he called up Sunder; they had not had the best of terms and had maintained distance from each other. He was distraught but not naïve, he knew no favor was done without expecting anything in return, but as long as Sunder could help he was ready to play by his rules.

Sunder had just returned from the party and was suitably drunk, when he got a call from a familiar but unsaved number, too exhausted he just grunted and ignored it, but it rang again, could be important.

"Hello"

"Sir!" Sorry to hear about your daughter"

"Yes I was just telling the commissioner that I have plenty of experience in dealing with such people, you know how politics has become these days"

"I know you are a great guy, few of the most valuable people of the city, of course I will help you"

"I have to be somewhere early morning; I will see you at 11, ok?"

"Don't worry everything will be fine, come over to my farmhouse, such things are better discussed away from the noisy city"

"No, there is no need to bring your wife; we will all party together once the little one is back"

"Try and get some sleep, good night"

After the call, Sunder called up Yash and informed about his meeting the next day, warning them to not drop the ball and keep Keira safe; the mood at the hideout was almost festive, everybody was sure that they will get the money, obviously not the amount that they had purposely quoted but enough to splurge it for a nice, long time to come.

Yash and Karan had come down to the warehouse with booze from one of their stashes and everybody partied till early morning. Keira was sedated with cheap Benadryl so that she didn't yell or throw a tantrum, she was just a victim of her father's greed after all and her being alive and well was mandatory for their future, they knew well that if things went downhill they would be on their own but if they worked out they will get a lot of money and power that they yearned for.

Karan had not been home in months. He called up once a week and talked about him being busy. He had partially told his parents about getting into real estate but had not mentioned that he didn't have a job yet. The parents didn't ask much but were satisfied when he told the kind of money he would earn even if one flat or piece of land was sold! How tough could that be in the city with so many people needing a house? Truth was that Karan didn't go home because he couldn't face his parents anymore. He knew they won't approve of what he does and the kind of people he hangs out with. But dad was old fashioned, there was no point explaining to him the ways of the world. The only way to be rich, famous and powerful was the way that he had chosen, only the weak and the coward labeled it the wrong way because they didn't have the guts to do it. Sometimes he wished his dad was like Yash's who didn't bother too much about his son. Yash had not been home for a while; he rarely called and sometimes sent some money home just for the effect. He was sure that his parents loved him but they knew that their son is not in school anymore and can take care of himself, his father would have understood had he seen his son's beer belly recently, it's all for the best.

They sat there, thinking that even if the deal comes down to a Crore, a hundred times less than what they had asked for, they would still be rich as the money only needed to be divided three ways; Yash, Karan and Raja were supposed to get most of the money while all the helpers will get fifty thousand each they had been secretly promised. Raja had made the call and besides the three of them, only Sunder was aware of the money that was asked for.

The meeting with Sunder had been bittersweet; it had begun at 11 and gone on till 7 in the night, but had given VK hope which none of the meetings with the police had done. The news was old for the media now and only appeared as a small column filled with rumors and fatal conclusions. VK was in no mood to drive and his spare driver was busy driving people of the family who had come over to offer condolences, though he hated the idea but he asked Jagan to drive him. He was angry at the driver but reasoned that it was an accident and could have happened to anyone, anyway, there were other more important things on his mind; his grief had taken over his temper for the time being. Jagan was embarrassed himself and drove VK to the farmhouse where he waited and chatted up with the guards. Sunder's farm house was bigger than VK had imagined, it looked like a place that was specially designed for secret deals and closet deeds. There was a large, well maintained pool outside with what looked like a stage in the center, surely for Russian dancers and other equally sleazy entertainment programs that the leader was rumored to enjoy, but nobody had the balls to cover his party and qualify the vine. Sunder offered VK expensive scotch, limited edition by noon which VK declined but took it after much request and believing that it will take the edge off the day and as a businessman he knew that negotiation needs patience. Sunder gave VK examples of help that he had rendered to people in cases that were beyond the reach of the law. He named some people, influential ones, who had asked him for help in cases of extortion, kidnapping and death threats and insisted that he should not just believe what he says but verify it from the people who were benefited. It had been two hours since he came and they had not really talked about their plan of action which irritated VK the businessman, but VK the father listened patiently, he had no other choice. Suddenly, VK could sense a perceptible change in Sunder's tone; from empathetic it became a little more businesslike, and said that he didn't do this as public service but so that he could get something in return. VK readily agreed to such a point, after all nobody would do things without serving their interest, he had expected that a slimeball like Sunder will ask for money or to fund his campaign or gift him a house. "Do you remember that small piece of land we had fought over?" And nothing more needed to be said; VK thought about the demand for a while, he cursed his stars for forcing him to beg to a guy who would not miss any opportunity to get what he wanted, even if it's at the expense of someone's misery. But this was not the time to haggle, he knew the loss to him would be much bigger than the ransom he is trying to negotiate but with him involved there was a better chance of finding his daughter than without him.

"Take your time to think over it", Sunder insisted but there was none. "You will have the papers by day after tomorrow evening and I will arrange for the transfer of the property to you, I can't do it any sooner, but please make sure that my daughter is not hurt in any way till then, I have already given you my word that I will keep my part of the deal with you." VK said coldly; Sunder smiled and extended his hand from where he sat on the couch and shook VK's limp hand with all the enthusiasm of a young boy. "I trust you", and with that he got up. VK couldn't think of anything, the meeting had still not been satisfactory, he was just going to ask Sunder about his plan when Sunder turned towards him, he put a hand on his shoulder. "You don't have to worry anymore; I will talk to these guys the next time they call you, chances are they will call you at the same hour that they did the last time, I shall be at your residence by 11 tomorrow night, and don't worry I know such people, they will keep her safe till their demands are met".

VK got a call at 11:30, Sunder received it.

"Hello"

"My name is Sunder, if you don't know me, ask around, they will give you my introduction."

"The girl you have kidnapped is my brother's daughter; you will get the money but not as much as you are asking for, don't ask for something that can't be done. The daughter's father won't be able to arrange that kind of cash and his daughter is a liability to you right now."

"Quote a number and I will make sure the payment is done but don't hurt the girl. No, still too high, I will give you 1 Cr for all your hard work; further negotiation can hurt both of us. No, fine we will wait."

The call was disconnected while VK looked with disbelief. It looked as if he was bargaining for vegetables, from 100 to 1; he could have tried and arranged earlier despite the current business cycle losses, he would have sold some land at a loss, but waiting for another call! Sunder looked at VK's troubled face and the sadist in him felt satiated; he grinned. "Don't worry they will call back, I do this for a living… in a way. We need to give them some money so that your daughter doesn't get hurt, I am trying to negotiate and wear them off as much as possible so that the amount can be smaller and arranged easily, as soon as I get the papers I will give you a call, don't take me wrong but I can't help you till I have the papers, business you see and rest assured the abductors will not dare to harm Keira now, she will get 5 star treatment till she get back. Anyway, I will be out of town for the next 2 weeks, I have been summoned for an urgent party meeting in Delhi, can't skip that..even for you."

VK just had to suppress his anger and nod solemnly; there was no choice but to wait for the call. But Sunder wasn't lying about the meeting part, to his concern, he had been asked to come over to Delhi for a week long team meeting which had forced him to put this plan on hold, he reluctantly had to leave the girl with his people for a period that was too long for his comfort, another week, he had just added to harass the egoistic bastard.

———◆•◆•◆———

Chapter 21

Top Gear

While VK was at the farmhouse the entire day, Jagan sat around first checking out the place and then chatting up with the staff. They informed him that the farm house belonged to Sunder and he held most of his meetings and all of his parties here. The name sounded largely familiar, he thought for a while and then it clicked him, he recalled having heard this name from Yash and Karan. He had not heard from either of them since the accident and he was anxious to know their version of the story. He knew he was not in a position to confront their master and ask him for their details, he might refuse or get him killed just because he could; he had become wary of people like him.

On the night of negotiation, it had already been 4 days since Keira had disappeared, on the excuse of buying some medicines; Jagan borrowed the guard's bike and followed Sunder back to his farm house. He didn't expect much from this adventure but half hoped to see the guys there. He rode cautiously maintaining distance and making sure that the night camouflages him well, his shoulder still ached but the knowledge of how he got hurt seemed more important than the hurt itself. After riding without the lights and just following the tail lights of the Scorpio for thirty long minutes, he could notice that the vehicle was slowing down; he stopped and watched the silhouette of the SUV wait for the guard to open the gate as it rolled in. He parked the bike on the side of the road and decided to walk. Sudden cease of an unfamiliar silencer might give him away, so he sneaked towards a vague direction forward. There was grit and the surface was uneven, he tumbled and fell face first on the ground, the fall only broken by his palms, his worn and injured body cursed him for this misadventure. He thought of leaving but then he saw one more vehicle approach the gate from the opposite end with speed. He limped rapidly behind the outline of a tree and stood there, the wall was high but he could see from above it if he stood on top of some kind of a platform, he could have gone in as the guard knew him now but didn't want his name to come up in some conversation. Using his new cell phone that he had bought from his savings from a market that was famous for selling second hand and stolen goods (his was not stolen); he looked for a few bricks or flat stones.

———◆·◆·◆———

There was some kind of a party going on, the glow of lights and moving heads could be seen, he could listen to the songs being played on some kind of a system and the hum of chatter, he decided to wait for a while.

The similarity was obvious, the jacket and thick facial hair couldn't hide the gait and confidence with which he walked. He had put on a few pounds and looked broader but it was definitely Yash, two more men followed him but he didn't know who they were. Surely he could go and meet his 'friend' but this didn't seem to be the time, this was not the place. Jagan pushed his bike a little further, sat on it, moved it with his legs and then kick started it; there was a lot of thinking to be done.

Over the next few days, unaware of the dealings taking place in the master's house, Jagan made sure that he never missed a chance to hover around that farmhouse, Yash surely didn't live there, he and his friend must be having a house and he will reach there eventually; he thought of asking the guys at the liquor store but decided against it, surely they will be told of his asking around. VK was too occupied to worry about Jagan's outings, he had stopped going to office and he looked like a pale imitation of his old self.

One night while leaving the liquor store, Jagan caught glimpse of a familiar face. He was on the bicycle of the gardener today, following a bike on by pedaling was going to be a killer but he needed answers, besides he was sure that nobody remembered him anymore least of all expect him to be voluntarily carrying out a bicycle chase. The chase barely lasted 15 minutes, which was a good thing; he would have either died of exhaustion or fallen in front of an oncoming bus. Karan carelessly parked the bike a little off the middle of the street and laboriously walked towards a middle aged building, there were stairs to the side of it that led to the upper floor without disturbing the residents on the ground floor, a typical arrangement in houses designed to be let out to tenants. Not much attention was paid to security; who could be interested in lower middle class people with barely passable accommodation? Jagan waited till he couldn't see Karan over the flight anymore then he tiptoed upstairs; his mind was beyond worrying about consequences, there were barely a couple dozen high stairs and soon he found himself on the top floor which had a couple of small 1 BHKs. The first one had no lights on, perhaps still up for rent but the other had a door open, must be guys waiting for the bottles. There could be a lot of drunken people who might pounce on him but he needed answers, he halted only for a while and jumped straight at the door before it got shut. For a

149

moment there was silence as the two occupants of the room stared blankly at the new arrival. Karan wasn't there and for a moment Jagan thought that he had mistaken or missed a turn, but there were no other floors or doors to take. The silence was broken by an elated Yash; "Jagan, you are alive! I am so happy to see you", Jagan thought he had seen the other guy who looked at him blankly while making a drink but right now he was more interested in meeting his old friends. Suddenly a narrow door opened, and Karan stepped out, for a moment he stood transfixed, looking at Jagan, rooted to the spot with his hands still wet. Yash noticed Jagan looking behind him, he broke the uncharacteristic embrace and walked to Karan with a big smile on his face; "look who is here Karan, didn't I tell you not to worry about our friend, I was sure he wouldn't die so early, Raja make him a drink man, cheers to Jagan." Jagan didn't know how to react, he didn't know what he expected but it wasn't this, he tried to refuse a drink but later yielded to Yash's pleas and an offer for free drinks. "It was all over the papers man, the accident", Karan joined in once some neat whisky got into his system. "We called you so many times but your phone was not reachable, must have been lost in that accident, no?" Jagan only partially heard the guys speak as his face oscillated between the two happy faces. "I know what you are thinking", Yash said, with a serious note in his voice, the room fell silent. "You must have cursed us for not getting in touch with you; we wanted to, you can ask anybody here, but the news of that girl going missing made us decide otherwise, you know how pig lazy cops turn into hunting dogs as soon as something happens to the rich guys; anyway! Enough about us, I sincerely hope that you understand, we were helpless, tell us your story, did you get hurt?" Jagan could sense some sincerity in Yash's voice; he told them the story, how he had hoped that he will hand over the girl to them before the truck driver knocked him out senseless for half a week and how the lost girl is being tracked vigorously by the police. For some reason, he didn't mention his brief visit to the farmhouse of Sunder Sharma. They drank that night, hoping that Jagan will speak while Jagan waited for them to drop a clue, neither happened.

There was not much left to do post the kidnapping, VK usually left with the police or other people to places he didn't want Jagan to come while his wife usually stayed home, she had begun looking much older than she was in just a month. Jagan had been visiting Yash and Karan more often and had forced them to get him a job elsewhere, the guys took a few days but he kept on pestering them and then one day they took him to meet Sunder. The leader knew everything about him, more than he remembered telling Yash and Karan. He knew his past, his stint with

VK, his near fatal crash and also about his family history, which though inconsequential, conveyed the point that his background had been thoroughly swabbed and analyzed. For the time being he was supposed to be a part of a fleet of five drivers who were permanently employed by Sunder for driving his people and for other miscellaneous assignments that needed dedicated and slightly dimwitted manpower.

It had only been less than a week and Jagan got a chance to prove that he had it in him to advance to the inner circle. He was driving Sunder back from his farmhouse after a usual night of women and booze. Everybody else had departed and Sunder had to be at home for an early morning meeting. It was dark and hazy, the road was quiet, preparing for the whole day of abuse and smoke, there were no oncoming lights or rashly moving heavy vehicles. Jagan gently eased the vehicle off the service lane on to the main road; the ongoing extension of the highway had made the path treacherous and unsafe for those who were unfamiliar with that two kilometer stretch. There was quiet, only broken by the sole radio station playing some random nineties songs to keep the driver awake. Sunder was napping in the back of the car; the booze had stopped working long ago, now it was just a habit, a pastime. "Go slow, it can be…", before Sunder could complete his advise the sedan went into a tailspin, Jagan couldn't do much but try and hold on to the steering and pray that like the last time the car stays on its wheels and doesn't go turtle, it was too late and too dark, there was nobody in sight, the shops were closed and the police station was far away; Jagan didn't have his phone and Sunder's was in his pocket but Jagan wasn't sure if he was alive. The impact was tremendous and the car skidded all the way to the side of the road that was dug up as a part of the ongoing development work undertaken by the corporation, the construction company was funded by Sunder and it would be an irony if he died by falling in that ditch dug by the agency. They did fall; the car fell sideways into a makeshift drain but got stuck due to uneven ground. The driver's door faced the ground; the other side was heavily damaged. Jagan struggled with the handle and the door gave way, he fell on the all too familiar grit. But it was just him, Sunder was still in the car and there was no sign of struggle from within. Jagan looked around for help, still shaken from is second near death experience in less than a year, maybe it was time to look for a safer job, but that later. He tried to slide beneath the car stuck sideways and open Sunder's door but it was locked from inside. Was he dead, this can't be happening; he would be in deep trouble if the man died. He hurriedly climbed out to the road, the back door of the car was smashed inside and couldn't be opened, and the front door was locked as well. Jagan got back into the ditch and tried getting back in the car from his side, the door was still ajar and he had to really use his strength to pull himself up on now an almost vertical seat, he tried to peep behind and he could see Sunder unconscious with his head resting on his side of the door. It was too dark to see the damage and Jagan unlocked the back door by pulling on the latch; it was easy and as soon as he did that Sunder's flaccid body fell off like a rag doll.

CHAPTER 22

CRISS CROSS

If there was a trait that Sunder appreciated the most and openly was somebody's willingness to die for him. With his heroics and struggle Jagan had stumbled into Sunder's most trusted brigade, the fact that the driver didn't steal 5 Lacs from his pocket even when he was unconscious got him even more favor points, not that Jagan knew there was money. Had he known, the story may have ended differently, but there was no certain way of knowing that.

For the time being, Jagan had shifted to the parking lot of Sunder, it was not as comfortable as his old place of work but was livable and here he felt more respected. That night he had to go on an errand with Yash, somewhere out of the city but like most times the details were withheld till the last moment, you just can never be too cautious when dealing with people of your kind. It was 10 pm, two hours later than the discussed time. An unmarked car stood outside the gates, Jagan had not seen it before and assumed that Sunder's men used this vehicle for carrying out activities south of the rulebook. It was a Thar, suitable for getting into villages not connected by roads. Jagan got into his seat and was accompanied by Yash, on the two rows in the rear sat Karan and Raja. "To the farmhouse", Yash said; Jagan didn't ask much. The traffic had thinned down and the frequency of the route was such that he could drive with eyes closed. Once they reached the farmhouse Jagan slowed down; "Keep going till the toll and take the narrow lane to its right." There was a sharp U-turn right before the toll booth, the lane was unlit and could only be faintly seen through the headlights. Jagan hesitated; "Go on, we won't kill you, we need a driver", Karan chided from behind. Jagan ejaculated a hollow laugh. They entered the *kachcha* lane, just about the width of the vehicle. The wild bushes objected to the entry of the heavy machine in their area and tried their best to prohibit the entry by madly lashing against the green beast. This was a first for Jagan but the rest looked like they had been here, they ducked comfortably till the vegetation thinned down after about 200 meters and the path widened. It was not a dead end but path to a village that seemed untouched by the city that was not too far from it.

They stopped outside what looked like the silhouette of a deserted building. It was just past midnight and other than a few curious village dogs that lost interest quickly, nobody was aware of the silent approach of the city ride. Jagan was the last to jump out; Yash had dialed a number but disconnected it after a couple of rings. After about ten minutes a guy appeared with a small torch which he only switched on when he was just a yard away from them, Jagan wasn't aware of his approach, "very sneaky", he appreciated the guard's stealth, just to pass some time and keep his mind occupied. No one else seemed to share his enthusiasm; the novelty must've worn off by now. No time was wasted on civilian niceties and guys just turned and followed the torch bearer, they entered through a small door; Jagan couldn't make out if they were at the front or rear of the building but this was not the time to think about such trivial matters, he could feel that he was a part of something important.

"Is she up?" Yash asked nobody in particular as soon as all were inside and the door was shut behind them, he exuded that aura of a boss and the rest submitted to him. "It is time for a surprise! Come with me", Yash nodded at Jagan with a sly smile and walked towards the corner that was dimly lit with a very weak bulb. "Switch on some light"; A guy brought a bright torch used in the farms, it looked like a small halogen lamp that lit up the entire corner that Jagan was now facing.

It had been a while since Sunder had last conducted a (staged) conversation with the abductors but no confirmation call had come yet. VK was getting nervous. Sunder had had to go out of town for a month at the behest of some party work which he couldn't have turned down and things were in an uncomfortable status quo.

The intercom rang; "What is it?"

"Who?"

"What does he want?"

"Fine!" Frisk him and send him upstairs."

The door opened and the guest walked in. VK lay on the couch that was close to the bar. His wife and daughter had been sent to his in-laws; he had become excessively paranoid and had been taking therapy, he feared losing the entire family now and had lain off a lot of his old staff.

"Didn't the accountant clear your salary?"

"He did".

"Then? What do you want"?

———————◆●◆———————

The party work had stalled Sunder for longer than he would have liked. There were pending matters back in the city and they could easily go out of control.

At night, he had called up the guys from the circuit house. They were going to be on the way to the warehouse; the new driver was taking them in the unmarked SUV he had taken as a gift from a business associate.

At the warehouse, the mood had become light once Jagan had seen the girl. The whole incident had been amusing just because of the look on the poor driver's face.

When he had walked to the corner with Yash, he half expected cash, weapons or drugs but it had turned out to be Keira. Of course! He thought to himself but nothing came out of his mouth, she lay there exhausted from the cries and dirty, scared to open her eyes and look at the people around her. In that moment, he felt ashamed of even fictitiously plotting it with these screwed up people; his jaws tightened out of anger, more at himself than at anybody else, the image of Yash grinning and feigning ignorance about the accident flashed in front of his eyes, but he couldn't speak, he had chosen sides. He turned towards Yash, who was grinning. Surprised? "That day when you got hit by that truck, we were right behind you, we could have rescued you, but there were way too many people and if we had not acted that day, we would've missed on a chance to pick her up, and don't take us wrong, we did check on you, you were just passed out, nothing serious; we were sure you would be taken care of; now you can't hold that against me! Besides now there is so much money that we are going to get! All of us, you won't have to work for anybody ever again. Imagine that! You are getting the money and revenge without doing any real work, lucky man."

Jagan wanted to say so much, choke the bastards who thought that he was expendable, that they could just run him over and take the girl away but now was not the time, he didn't know if ever he would get a chance but this was not it. "*Chal* now, forget about it"; it was Karan's turn to derail the driver's train of thought; "You'll have to drive back to the city to get some booze and food, it is time to celebrate your newfound knowledge and wealth, and don't forget to pick up some *ganja* from Ali's."

Chapter 23

Sleepless Night

There was no time. After what the driver had told him, VK had no time to wait or weigh his options. He had to act and act fast, but who could be trusted, certainly not the police. Too much delay would ruin his chances of meeting his daughter alive, let alone rescuing her from the bastards; Sunder would be back to the city on Monday, he had less than a week to carry out the operation. After that he would get his daughter back but in return of a lot of money and forever gratitude towards the two faced snake who had laid such an elaborate plan for a piece of land.

After a lot of deliberation, debates and self doubt he decided to involve the police at the highest level so that the news doesn't leak out, there was somebody who might help him but VK's past with him had been patchy to say the least, but the consequences of collaborating with an unreliable cop could be terrible. He went through his archaic card holder and searched for a number he never wanted to call up.

Sudheer Kulkarni used to be a close buddy of VK in school, both studied together, played tennis together and dreamed of becoming big officers, but as is the case with most such friendships, with time they had parted ways; VK had taken the way up compromising with the values while Sudheer enrolled himself in the police services and took a lengthy and painful path, made tougher with his inflexible attitude towards corruption and such similar necessary evils. He still lived in government quarters, had not minted money or created infinite property like his contemporaries and even juniors. His wife, Suman, was a content soul as well, perfect for a man like him, often men have an excuse of their family to take up to unscrupulous ways but not this man, he had a son but VK didn't know much about him, must be preparing for or pursuing some fair, lawful, inconsequential career, VK thought for a moment.

The landline number rang, even a completed ring seemed to be taking minutes; the number must have changed, what if he has been transferred, what if he isn't there and his wife doesn't recognize me, what if he decided to purposely ignore me; VK wanted to hang up but the father waited. He didn't have Sudheer's cell phone number but even if he had, he would have called up on the landline hoping they didn't have a caller ID

After an agonizingly long wait, just when he was about to put the receiver down and begin flipping through the deck, the voice answered.

"Hello"

"Ya, speaking, who is this?"

"VK! Who?"

"Oh! Wow, how are you?"

"It has been so long, it was just yesterday that Suman and I were talking about you; good that I was home today for lunch else would've missed your call."

"I thought you were handling it your way, I really didn't want to get into it and trouble you, you know."

"Oh! Hmm"

"Come over tonight at about 10, have dinner with me."

"No formalities, you are an old friend, I'm glad you thought of me."

"See you tonight, bye"

VK drove to the officer's bungalow himself. He wanted to reach as soon as he hung up but that would have been futile. He hung around, downing a few, and then drove slowly but still reached a little early; time has a funny way of moving.

It had been about ten years since that fight. VK was just starting out as an entrepreneur and had gotten into a disagreement with certain members of the union. A scuffle had metamorphosed into a brawl and few people were gravely injured. Most of the guilty belonged to VK's team, he had tried to use Kulkarni as a shield but Sudheer had refused leading to long drawn court case against him; VK had caught the officer by his collar and abused him while Sudheer had maintained his calm hoping that VK will understand his duties as an honest officer. It had been the beginning of a communication background; now more mature and world wise, VK could see how wrong he had been and how by not apologizing he had been even more wrong, but it was too late now, just because he needed help he couldn't manipulate a guy who had agreed to help a greedy idiot like himself and still had sounded more genuine than Sunder.

House was modest but neat, Suman *bhabhi* had opened the door; Sudheer was unmarried when the incident happened and VK had ignored his wedding invitation but she had been his childhood sweetheart, so he hoped that she didn't know much about the incident. He rang the bell just once, hoping that nobody opens the door so he can go back. It was the most awkward that he had felt in a really long time, he was used to prowling in his own territory. Suman opened the door and smiled, just like the old times, she looked the same too. She wore a modest Saaree and invited him in. Sudheer wasn't there.

"He is in the bathroom, getting ready; he just got back from work."

"Can't help it, he has always been hard working", VK added lamely; such social gatherings had become a thing of the past, he only interacted with people for work or with an intention of getting work done, such guileless conversations made him feel fidgety.

"Nice house", he added. Suman smiled and the following silence of a few seconds was loud; only broken by the squeak of the bathroom door.

"Well you are on time, for a change! I thought I won't see you before 11", entered Sudheer smiling wearing an ironed white *kurta pajama*. VK got up with arms frozen to his side, sweaty palms. Sudheer hugged him; "relax, this is not your big meeting, you can drop the formality." VK grinned idiotically and sat down next to Sudheer while Suman went to the kitchen.

———◆◆◆———

Sunder was not happy; not that he wasn't gaining by being away from the city but because he wasn't present back home, especially when there was so much at stake. He never doubted that he had employed fools who could fuck up even the simplest of things either by being drunk, high or by assuming that they were smart. He told them and they did it exactly like they were instructed and that's how it worked, that's how it had been working for him for years.

He had begun his political career as a henchman cum driver for a big local leader and then eventually due to his willingness to do anything to become a favorite and a commendable lack of conscience he had risen up the ranks; first in the inner circle then on the margins of the hoardings that peppered the city throughout the year and then in the centre with the big guns. He had cleverly manufactured a façade, that of the messiah of the poor who would do whatever he could to not let the tax evading rich mistreat the employees. This has won him a clear fan following amongst the rickshaw drivers, cart pushers and other such men who considered him as one of them, the one who would help them gain money, power or fame merely by association.

He now sat in the party office, bored of the meeting, his mind back at the warehouse. He did talk yesterday, the guys sounded cheerful enough, must be drunk, fools! There was going to be a dinner tonight and he wouldn't be able to call them, there won't be much privacy, his train of thought was suddenly derailed by a mention of his city.

It was going to be a quick sting operation, to be headed by five officers in plain clothes. This was not the first time that Sudheer had heard a kidnapping story and involvement of Sunder in brokering the deal, but he knew VK had given him a chance that he had been waiting for. Guys like Sunder were many and when one went down, somebody else ascended the ladder but it was important to intervene and cleanse from time to time, isn't that the *dharma* of people like him.

Sudheer knew Sunder's itinerary, he would be back to the city on Monday morning and the operation must be carried out before that, the abductors needed to be killed, negotiations won't work; make it look like a fight that broke out within the gang members and they shot each other, not unheard of, rescue the girl, tell the press that she was found tied behind the bushes as the kidnapper fled the scene and cause minimum damage to his team and himself.

Sunder had sounded nervous, there was nothing new about it, he always behaved this way when he went off for some party work. Yash was instructed that all members stay at the warehouse at all times till he arrived, he didn't want to take any chances and be followed. Send Jagan, an unknown face; to fetch food and other requirements, and most importantly, keep the girl alive and healthy, her well being was the ticket to their bright future.

There was this entire weekend to enjoy in this shitty warehouse. No television, no girls, only booze and cards to pass time. The unimportant guys had already left, only Yash, Karan and Raja remained behind, accompanied by the two guards who were permanently stationed there till things concluded. All of them carried guns, unregistered but handy in case of a blowout. Besides the guards, only Raja had used the gun in real life, Yash had fired in the air once to see how it feels while Karan had just watched and fantasized about shooting it.

It was only 8 pm but appeared like midnight. There were no villagers around. Surprisingly enough for Karan, the guys had never bothered finding out what goes on in that huge building, not more than five hundred meters of any of their houses; pathetic or smart? He couldn't tell. They knew well enough not to poke nose in the business of the powerful; the righteous, muscular heroes only existed on pirated CDs, thankfully. There was a time when he fantasized about being one, who aspires to be the bad guy after all! But then, he reasoned silently, there are no rewards for being a good guy; not enough money, no power, no respect. Today when they moved, people and the law avoided them. Isn't this the life that one dreams of? Then what's the point of being how your parents asked you to be. But the thought of parents derailed his train of thought. He suddenly felt somber and sad, didn't know why. The disapproving and disappointed face of his dad hovered in front of him while the helpless yet supportive voice of his mother echoed in his ears; "don't be so harsh on him, one day he will make us all proud". She was so wrong, he thought. But not really, nobody cares once you get into the big league; everybody just wants to stand besides you and get pictures clicked. And he was close, just this deal and it will all change, he could bet bigger, he would be known as one of the few who pulled off such a big scandal without any fuck up; more respect, more money.

Yash lay on his side, not as peaceful as Karan. Success of this assignment would get him money, but it was power that he desired. Power was the key to all the locks in the world; the key to all the banks and all the 'VIPs only' lounges. But, a million things could go wrong, what if the girl dies, what if Sunder compromises them if need arises, what if the cops, or worse, VK sniffs them out; he never underestimated that guy, begrudgingly respected him for what he was and the respect that he commanded in the city without being a *neta* or a don. What if they get caught, the trust of his dad in him would be broken, and he would probably spend a long time behind the bars with no money or no lawyer to bail him out.

He must be ready at all times, nobody could be trusted. The ones around him were fools, too easy to manipulate, but not him, he must have a plan B, he had a plan B.

Raja was asleep. He didn't care much about anything or anybody anymore. A quarter of whisky and joint helped him sleep well. Since that day, it was as if his soul had left him, he was not the funny guy anymore. Nothing interested or repulsed him, he just went on, doing what was told. What if he died tomorrow? Good riddance to bad rubbish! He didn't feel loyal to anybody anymore, at first there was Yash, but then he became a little distant after the incident, Sunder rescued him but now he was pretty sure he did it to get a hired gun that would fire as long as it could and then be replaced when it becomes, unstable.

———◆———

CHAPTER 24

WINDING UP

After the initial meeting, Jagan had only met VK once with Sudheer, it was agreed that there was a threat of him being tailed and followed back to the house; in Sunder's absence, the chances were slim but a possibility could not be ruled out. He visited one of the three liquor stores decided by the day, where one of the three cops met him to gather developments and give him further instructions. It was dangerous, there could be other people watching, other double agents in the force couldn't be ruled out but Jagan had to take that risk; earlier it was only the urge to avenge his accident but since he had seen Keira it had become an act of redemption as well. The short rendezvous, never exceeding five to seven minutes were kept as random as possible; sometimes it was an exchange while creating a parking space, or sometimes on the pretext of urinating near the bushes. No phone numbers were exchanged and it had to be a chanced visit.

Sunder felt uneasy, he decided to feign sickness and depart a couple of days earlier. The flight was supposed to depart from Delhi at about 6 in the evening and touch down by 7:30, a short journey but bad weather delayed the flight by 3 hours. Sunder was increasingly getting nervous. Unlike his hometown, he didn't have five people to schmooze and keep him happy, he was alone, his PA had stayed back on the orders of the seniors and anyways he had to do this alone. He felt as if something had gone wrong but couldn't explain this anxious feeling. It could be withdrawal symptoms of being away from his territory, but he had an important business to finish, if not for a sudden call from the party chiefs, he would have been a richer man with a stronger PR, network and good press that even his seniors would envy, it was about network after all.

The set piece was complete. Jagan had informed the team about the location and a brief reconnoitering exercise had marked a point of entry from an end opposite to the one where the hostage and the guards were active. The small iron door at the other end of the warehouse was identical to the one that was used by the guys but was locked shut with an old padlock, rusted, with keys lost long ago. Invisible in the night, the guards didn't find it worth guarding even during the day, days of inaction had made them complacent. Whenever Jagan got a chance to wander outside for a smoke or to voluntarily check on a noise, he would try and loosen the screws so that the door could be opened with a strong shoulder if need be. The plan was simple, the five men would enter the clearing post 10 pm and wait behind the bushes till they got some kind of a signal from Jagan. It could be flicker of a light or that of a matchstick thrice if a torch wasn't available. Jagan would go back to the hideout and do nothing. The team will split with two watching the front while the three will use the weakened back door to enter the warehouse. As there were no eyes inside, the rest of the plan was tentative. Jagan was supposed to be positioned in an area closer to Keira; saving her was the primary target of the mission. If the inhabitants drew out guns and tried to engage the team, they had orders to shoot them on the spot, remove the bodies and shift the crime scene to an area that could be explained better to the higher ups and media without making it look like a well planned operation but a chance encounter. Sudheer wouldn't have approved of such MO but he knew that they weren't up against amateurs and a slip up could cause severe harm, not just professional.

He should have reached the city by now, Sunder thought but here he stood at the terminal, waiting for the plane to taxi to the departure gate. His phone was dead and he felt helpless without it. He had decided to drop in to the warehouse and give the boys a surprise, but the weather had fucked up everything. He didn't have any proof that something was going to go wrong and just by mouthing off to his men he didn't want to sound like he was getting weak or going senile, that was the first sign of preparing a successor who indulged in a coup to overthrow you, just the way he had done. Of the lot he knew that the one who wants to take his place is Yash, the bastard! Suddenly an unexplained rage rose against Yash in his mind; the paranoia and distrust made him think that he would plan to kill him if the chance arises. This was too much to take and he chided himself for distrusting his most valuable player right now; there was still an hour before departure, he decided to pass time at the bar and drink till his nerves settled.

———◆◆———

Sudheer fully knew that VK would not agree to stay back and wait for the operations to conclude. He had decided to accompany him in his car and park at least a 100 meters away from the spot where the trail to the village begun.

This operation was even hidden from the higher ups in the police because he knew that a lot of them regularly enjoyed gifts for silence from people like Sunder, so the cards had to be kept close to the chest. The 5 officers who were a part of the case were the ones he trusted the most for their sincerity and physical prowess and they had all been snubbed by the law on multiple occasions while trying to bring Sunder or his thugs to justice, leaving them insulted and frustrated. Sudheer was a cautious man, transferred around the country and kept out of political dealings because of his upright conduct, the kind that is desirable on paper but unwelcome otherwise, and now while doing something that might cost him his job or more, he had kept the identity of the men secret even from his friend, the guys were referred to as F1, F2, R1, R2 and R3 after the positions they were supposed to assume at the time of the raid.

It poured that night, the visibility was almost nil and the routine power cuts because of the storm had blacked out the streets. This could be an ideal time for a raid or suicide depending on how they played it, Sudheer thought.

All of Sunder's men, five of them were stuck inside the warehouse. It was dark and they could easily hear the sound of clouds and thunder. Heavy rains pelted the roof and it was awfully loud, time and again they could hear the boom of lightning hitting spots nearby, a common occurrence in open areas. The guards, bored of their duty by now had already decided to call it a day, they took orders from nobody but Sunder and even he hadn't called them that day so they had been lucky to find time to slack off and drink a little bit more before the boss returned and put them up to longer, thankless hours.

Jagan had put a carpet close to Keira, she had seen him and asked him for help but all he could do was ask her to eat a little and be happy, she would be gone soon. Yash and Karan had had a laugh witnessing the helpless ex employee. Keira had eaten a little and fallen asleep. It was dark and Jagan had no way of knowing the time. What if he got too late and the cops called off the operation, what if he fell asleep and fucked it up. He had to be up and awake.

Sunder's plane landed at 10:15 and he instantly felt at ease; this was his city, his kingdom, people looked at him and bowed; the staff, the kiosk owners, the taxi drivers, everybody wanted to please him and do that extra bit hoping that he would help them some day. He was weighing his options as to go home or go to the warehouse when he spotted his driver and the SUV. His PA must have called and informed about his changed hours, must give him a raise, he chuckled.

"Take me to the farmhouse", Sunder instructed the driver before even settling down in his seat. He flung the bag to the side and connected the phone to the charger. It was raining heavily. Even at such an hour, traffic seemed to be moving at snail's pace. This was a fucked up day he thought, he just hoped that it ended at this.

Once at the farmhouse, he let the driver go home. After hanging around, using the bathroom (he hated small toilets in the planes) and shooting down some scotch, he took the keys of his SUV to drive to the warehouse.

The operation was delayed a little. Rains had blocked some parts of the city, people walked outside their houses with water that was knee high. Power cuts and black outs in low lying areas had made the entire experience flood like. There were seven men in VK's van, one of the officers had driven it as he didn't have that good an eyesight and didn't even remember when was it last that he had driven one of these.

The mission would be tougher than they had thought, unlike the cops on TV, there were no infrared or nightvision glasses to help them conduct a suave operation; this was going to be messy.

Once they saw the signal from Jagan, it would take them at least 10 minutes to sneak to the back of the warehouse, making sure that they are not spotted and that there are no booby traps around. Once at the back, they only had to rely on his description of the weakness of the shackle and break it in one go so that those inside didn't get a chance to react or prepare themselves. The loud rain and thunder would help in covering the sound of their movements; the darkness would make their detection tough, but they couldn't use torches themselves at the risk of being discovered or alarming the kidnappers and they will have to sense their way across the building as stealthily as possible.

But first was the question of reaching on time, there had been an accident on the highway, a common occurrence in such weather and the van was stalled. With weapons and few equipments, they couldn't afford to walk all the way, it would be tiring and dangerous, so they waited. The operation had to be completed by night and there was still time. In case Jagan didn't signal, they would go all out and break in from both the ends hoping to nab the guys before the victim is harmed, but they hoped it didn't come to that.

On his way to the warehouse, the drunk and impatient Sunder had banged a small car sideways into the divider, his behemoth had only had some dents and he moved on, not worrying about the law as was his habit. He couldn't afford to waste time in such petty issues, not when there was something much bigger at stake. He had sped away not worrying about the stalling traffic behind and sounds of wailing and yelling by some idiots.

In ten minutes, he would go through those silly bushes and park his vehicle. It would be a hell of a surprise. Time to see how the guys utilize their time in the absence of their boss. The road was muddy and it was difficult to drive through, but he couldn't leave the vehicle on the road and walk through the swamp, in his current shape he will never make it, even if it was just a few hundred meters. As soon as he was about to clear the growth, he swerved to the right and killed the engines. He could see a silhouette of the warehouse. The guards were missing, lazy bastards must be sleeping inside like the rest of them, there was no light or sound, or maybe he couldn't hear it in this stupid rain. He was wearing a raincoat and carrying an umbrella and didn't want to fall sick to conclude the worst day of his life. He stumbled to the small door, his boots covered with mud, making his steps and breathing heavy; a soft knock and then he waited; no answer. Must have been because of the rains, he knocked harder, nothing. As usual the patience wore off faster than the booze; he kicked and abused whoever was inside. "Who is it?" Came an almost indiscernible whisper. "It is me, you fools", hissed Sunder.

------◆------

Jagan had been worried; he had no reason to go out in this godforsaken rainy night. He couldn't light up a matchstick, it was too damp for that, looking for a flashlight and taking it out might be suspicious so he lay there with his ear at the entrance, hoping that the guys didn't wait for his signal and just barged in to end it all. Suddenly he heard a faint knock, could be a rat, there were plenty of them around, some as big as a dog or it could be just his imagination and nerves, conjuring things up that he wished happened.

But then there was another, louder. The guards were definitely drunk and out, Yash and Karan didn't seem to move, they must have dozed off, weather was such. He fumbled for the torch that was right next to one of the overweight guards. He was snoring all the way to heaven, no wonder he couldn't hear anything. Taking the light, he tiptoed to the door. "Who is it?" He asked in almost a whisper, cops sure can't be that polite! Sunder's voice broke the little conversation in his head. He hurried to the door and opened it. Sunder pushed him and got in. It was pitch dark but he could make out some big bodies that had begun to move a little and he kicked one of them. "Get up you bastard"; All the sleeping men got to their feet at once, as if their subconscious had a registered memory of that hoarse voice. Yash, Karan, Raja and the two guards; it was tough to see their expressions but they must surely be that of shock and awe.

Amidst of all the yelling and swearing, Jagan got the chance that he was waiting for, not the perfect one but the only one. He moved the door to shut it then stopped, he turned politely towards Sunder and asked, "Sir, it seems one of the windows of the SUV is open, should I roll it up"? Hmm, Sunder grunted absent mindedly and passed the key in the darkness between him and the driver. Jagan picked it up from the floor and ran to the vehicle. With every 4 steps he furiously blinked the light, sure that nobody would be able to make it out on such a night and anyways everybody must be busy saving their ass right now.

———◆•◆•———

VK sat nervously while the van moved through diverted traffic, with no sirens, no preferences, just a rich man in an average car; he had to wait like everybody else. As they moved forward, they saw a red Nano, canted on the divider, nobody seemed dead but that car was the reason for the jam. The van now moved on the wrong side of the road, the right side for the operation. They moved slowly, and rolled to a stop at a deeper shoulder so that the parked van wouldn't obstruct traffic in any way. The men got down and disappeared in the bushes, leaving just Sudheer and VK. Now all they had to do was to wait and see how it goes.

The guys had disappeared in the bushes and moved forward rapidly, they had to make up for the lost time.

They were at the clearing with minutes; an SUV was parked in front of the warehouse. It was 11:35 and they waited for a signal. There weren't any communication devices or walkies and were on their own, because set on an open frequency the messages would have reached people they weren't supposed to reach. It must have been about ten minutes when they saw a light at the warehouse and it rapidly moved towards them, they stayed hidden. The man came to the vehicle, waited for a while and ran back; it was time.

———◆◆◆———

Sunder seemed a bit relieved. Everything had been fine but his surprise visit confirmed his fears. The guys had taken it a little too easy and this could have botched the entire exercise. His absence was to blame, but now he was back and it was time to wrap it up. The guys sat down and heard while Sunder spoke about the way forward. A call had to be made in the morning to VK, threatening him about the consequences as the things hadn't moved. He would call up Sunder who would reach by afternoon, another call would be made by 5 and rendezvous point would be decided, it was going to be a deserted village about 2 Kilometers from the warehouse.

———◆•◆•◆———

The stage was set; the 2 officers had positioned themselves to the left and right of the entrance while the 3 marched on to the back. The entire place seemed to be in a swamp and every step was getting heavier. Once at the rear of the warehouse, at six steps from the edge was the old door. The two officers drew out their guns and torch while the third one prepared to kick it open.

———◆•◆•◆———

The meeting was over and Sunder had asked Jagan to drive him back to the farmhouse. Jagan had not expected this, the entire mission could fail, he didn't even know if anybody had seen his signal. Just when he was about to comply, there was a thud, guys sharply turned towards the source of the sound. The guards had already drawn their guns and were running towards the back of the building, it could be nothing but they had to run anyway. Sunder was transfixed, this development had taken him by surprise and his first thought was to run away and then find out what really happened. There was nothing for a while. Jagan shined the light towards the opening, the gate seemed to be ajar and the guards had gone out and not come back.

———◆•◆•◆———

Thank God for the foolish goons, thought one of the officers as he heard footsteps of multiple people running towards them. The guys created a lot of noise and were waving flashlights, the beams of which moved wildly in the darkness making it easy to spot the incomers. Both the big buffaloes were shot in the head without any buildup, their flashlights had dropped right there, still lighting up the dark as if sending a weak bat signal.

———◆•◆•◆———

That was surely the sound of a gun, Raja said and the guys took their positions behind the wall. Only Jagan didn't have a gun and he slid towards the girl as inconspicuously as possible, pretending to be cowering with fear. 3 flashlights moved into the elongated space, seen from the other end. One fell straight on the face of Sunder who stood frozen in the center of the room while the others scoured the area.

"Game is up guys, drop your weapons, come out and get on your knees." This is right out of a movie, Karan kept on thinking, his legs were shaking and if not for the wall, he would have collapsed. The girl had gotten up and looked around wildly, clueless to her rescue operation. She tried to get up but was held by Jagan who helped her sit down; she was too weak right now. Yash replied from behind the wall, "listen piece of shit, whoever you are, that girl is still with us, do not forget that. Suddenly a bullet came flying towards him, shot by the trained officer judging from the direction of his sound; it whizzed past him as he was peeping from the side of the wall. He was shocked, all his candor seeping out of his pores in form of sweat. Jagan moved quickly, carrying Keira on his side and bolted towards the officers. Everybody was transfixed, Yash, Karan and Raja, nobody had noticed that Sunder had already exited the warehouse from where he had entered. Raja was the only one who gathered what happened, just the anger of betrayal made him come out and shoot calmly at the figure of Jagan who would be enveloped by the darkness soon. The men were clearly covering for Jagan, they could belong to some other gang who were actually abducting her from abductors, he didn't care, he aimed for Jagan's head and fired, confident that he won't miss. At the same moment two things happened, Raja had exposed himself for so long that the three officers aimed at him simultaneously, the bullets got him in the chest and the abdomen and he fell down to never get up again; in the meanwhile, another man had fallen down, Jagan while running for his life, half expecting somebody to shoot from behind stumbled over some old piece of hardware and crashed to the floor with Keira in his hand, this was the moment when Raja's bullet missed him by barely an inch. He didn't try to get up and half crawled out of the warehouse with Keira who was now awake and tightly holding on to him.

———◆•◆•◆———

As soon as Raja went down, Yash knew that he would be next, he blindly ran out towards the door expecting to disappear in the woods just like Sunder.

———◆•◆•◆———

The anticipation had become too much to take for VK and he begged Sudheer to leave the van and accompany him to the warehouse. The rain had let up a bit; Sudheer knew that it would be impossible to convince VK and he was anxious for his men too. They abandoned the vehicle and entered the forest moving as fast as they could.

All the five officers stood in a circle, there were two men in the center illuminated by 5 torch lights. One was a young guy, must be Yash, Jagan had briefed them about him being the leader of Sunder's gang and the other, to everybody's surprise, was Sunder himself. He was sweating and looked very angry. Till now both the men had not ruled out the possibility of the involvement of another gang but as soon as Sunder saw Sudheer and VK he was livid! "You bastards, you will pay for this, both of you and not just your daughter but now everybody will die; I had given you such a good deal you fool but you were too greedy, you will pay for this now and this eunuch friend of yours won't be much help either, by the end of the day tomorrow, he would be packing his bags to a godforsaken place that isn't even on the map." All this while, he kept staring just at the two late entrants, drooling like a rabid dog cornered at the end of the road, hands shaking. VK wanted to reply but Sudheer caught his hand.

"So you admit to being a part of this crime? You had planned the kidnapping? You must be aware that all your friends have died by now and this shit is too deep even for you to come out of. It's just the two of us here, this boy of yours, nobody knows him, he is a goner already, if you wish there can be another version of the truth." Sunder was now listening intently as Sudheer had hoped. "So I think you don't know this boy with you and you accompanied us to the site of kidnapping to rescue a respected businessman's daughter, you risked your life for the good of the people who selected you and put this criminal away for life, yes it won't be less than that, but it shouldn't worry you, you have an entire factory of bastards like him, no?"

The entire thing had taken Sunder by surprise, he was sure that his career was over and all the yelling was only a desperate effort to see if he could crack the officer and the rest would follow; his face softened. "We can work this out I suppose, he said smiling, criminals like him shouldn't roam around free, I will help you to get justice, you can keep the land too, I will give you protection and make sure that nobody in the city bothers you ever again".

Yash knew this would be coming, he stood there trembling in rage, he had known his boss way too well and knew that he won't even blink before sacrificing others for his own interests; he would have done the same but he had hoped that for all his services and complete support, Sunder won't give him away so cheaply, but he had, the snake. Yash's anger grew, he gave up everything for this guy, his friends died inside and he was carrying out the deal as nonchalantly as if selling his car. He yelled and before the officers could understand lunged at Sunder, choking him. For a while everybody froze and watched the action, suddenly there were gun shots.

———◆•◆•◆———

Karan had lain on the floor, the gun had fallen from his hand and his hands were shaking with fear. He had seen Raja die; Jagan the snake run away and Sunder the coward flee the scene leaving them there. When Yash made for the door, he wanted to flee, but was too scared to stand, he had lain on the floor, curled in the dark corner praying that nobody spots him. When everybody was outside, he had overheard the entire conversation and understood that Yash would be gone forever. In that moment, remembering all of Yash's favors, he had picked up his gun, cocked it like he was taught and ran outside. He knew there were few people and there was a good chance that he might succeed.

———◆•◆•◆———

As Karan began shooting, everybody fell to the ground; he was spraying bullets aimlessly, abusing nobody in particular and asking Yash to run. He made a line towards the trees like a mad man, shooting and yelling, his legs straining to cover the distance that had seemed to be lesser the last time. He could hear his heart beat in his ears and his heavy breathing, it was so loud that he didn't pay heed to the warning to stop, just a little more and he would disappear behind that large bush; before he could change his direction a bullet caught him in the small of the back and he went down with a thud, his scream piercing through the damp, quiet space. He could feel the warmth of the blood as he lay on his face, waiting to die; "so this is how it feels like to be shot", his mind raced. It was like the movies, he saw his mom, his dad teaching him how to ride a bicycle, him watching TV stretched on a couch, his friends whose face he couldn't really make out but they were laughing, Nayar was also laughing, how did he reach there? His breathing was labored and pain was too much to feel now, had he known he would die today; he would have called up his mom and hugged his dad once, fuck it!

Yash had seen Karan run, he wanted to stop him and make him surrender but he knew it was too late, too late for all of them. He had been an ok kid; not too bright but certainly not somebody who deserved to be shot down like a dead dog in the middle of nowhere, he deserved better. With everybody looking at the fleeing mad man, Yash took out the knife that Raja had taught him to carry in his boots. No, he can't kill the officers, it would be a waste of chance but he could kill him and he did, he cut Sunder's jugular and the boss gurgled and went down on the spot. He still had the knife in his hand when as a reflex one of the officers pressed the trigger and the bullet went right through his heart, thus concluding the rescue operation.

EPILOGUE

'**Sunder Sharma Stabbed, Critical, Police Kill the Perpetrators in An Encounter**', read the headlines in the evening news. The name of the hospital was kept hidden to avoid the flood of political supporters and activists and the next day he was declared dead in one of the hospitals that had VK as its chief trustee. The murderers were identified as Yash, Raja and Karan who used to be the leader's followers but had had fallout with him over some political issues.

Keira's news was never published and the papers were covered with the biggest murder controversy in months. Sudheer and his men were recommended for a promotion, while Jagan, who had stood by the side of the building with Keira in his hands till the bullet killed Yash had left the city. He wanted to go back to his town and start a new life. VK gave him Ten Lacs and forgave him for his role in the abduction. A new leader was elected, who sits in the party office where Sunder used to sit.